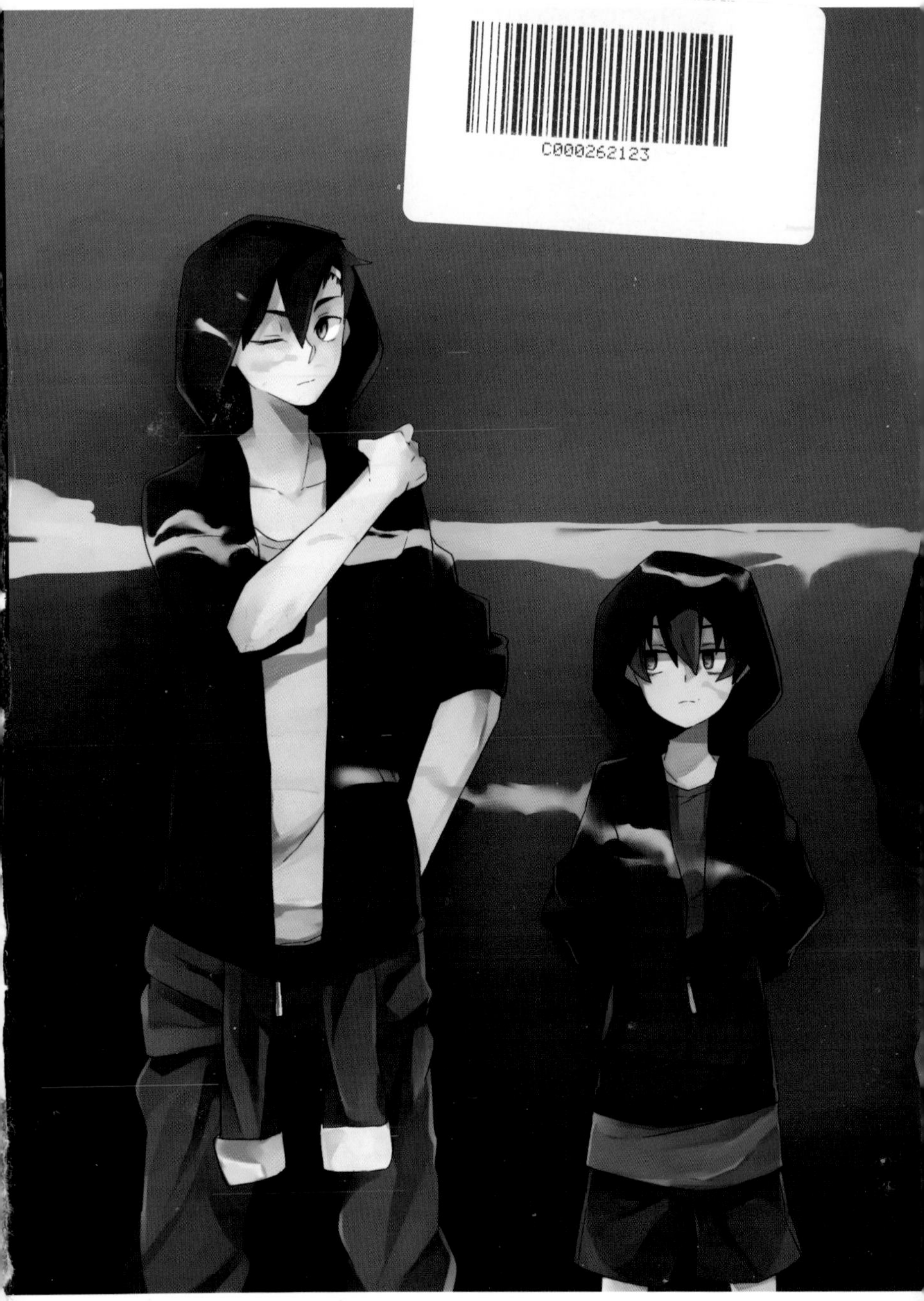

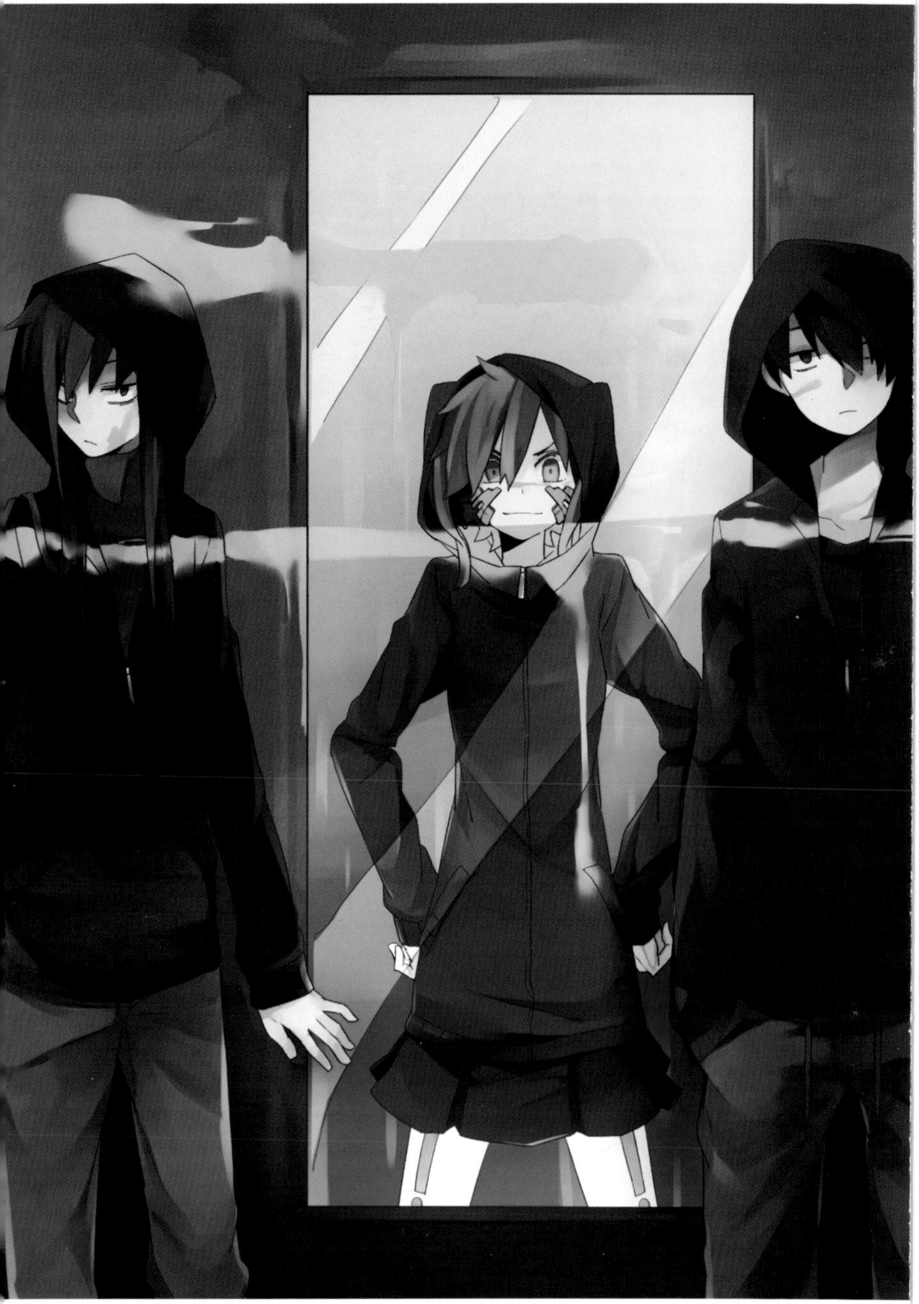

KAGEROU DAZE
VOLUME 2: A HEADPHONE ACTOR

JIN (SHIZEN NO TEKI-P)
ILLUSTRATED BY SIDU

YEN
ON

NEW YORK

KAGEROU DAZE, Volume 2
Jin (Shizen no Teki-P)

Translation by Kevin Gifford

Kagerou Daze II -a headphone actor-
©2012–2014 KAGEROU PROJECT/ 1st PLACE

Edited by BOOKWALKER Co., Ltd.

First published in Japan in 2012 by KADOKAWA CORPORATION ENTERBRAIN.

English translation rights arranged with KADOKAWA CORPORATION, Tokyo, through TUTTLE-MORI AGENCY, INC., Tokyo

Yen On
Hachette Book Group
1290 Avenue of the Americas
New York, NY 10104
www.hachettebookgroup.com
www.yenpress.com

Yen On is an imprint of Hachette Book Group, Inc. The Yen On name and logo are trademarks of Hachette Book Group, Inc.

The publisher is not responsible for websites (or their content) that are not owned by the publisher.

First Yen On edition: September 2015

ISBN: 978-0-316-34204-9

10 9 8 7 6 5 4 3 2 1

RRD-C

Printed in the United States of America

TABLE OF CONTENTS

HEADPHONE ACTOR I

Within the dim, dusky corridor, I stood, accompanied only by my shadow.

Until just a moment ago, I could hear the radio station leaking out from the headphones hanging around my neck.

Now all I could hear was noise. That, and something that resembled a person's voice.

Something had plainly changed. Concerned, I tried putting on my headphones.

—The crackling, intermittent voice slowly, gradually began to form coherent speech.

It sounded like a press conference held by the president of some country or other.

It was an exaggerated voice, affected for speech purposes, and a machinelike interpreter lagging a bit behind.

The static made listening difficult, but one could still manage to discern it.

"...It is with heartfelt regret that...by the...today...the Earth will...to an end."

When the voice came to a stop, it was greeted with a steady stream of shouting and seemingly meaningless gibberish.

Even through the headphones, the blubbering, panic-driven desperation of the audience was all too clear.

Beyond the red-tinged window, a large flock of birds had completely blocked the newly risen crescent moon from the deep violet sky, like a horde of black ants.

Removing my headphones and shooting a glance at the room I just left, I saw an abandoned video game and a mountain of study guides, both shining orange from the setting sun.

*   *   *

What was I doing up to now?

I had the impression I was speaking with someone until just a minute ago, but I couldn't even remember who.

"...This has to be some kind of joke."

I whispered it to myself, trying to will myself into believing it, as I opened one of the windows lining the corridor. I was greeted with a loud, shrill siren, like none I had heard before, along with the screaming and ranting of people.

The din steadily grew louder and louder, enveloping the entire city.

My lips quivered as my teeth clattered against each other.

I am alone.

There's nobody left here.

And before too long, I'll be gone, too.

My pulse raced. Tears flowed across my cheeks.

—I don't want to be alone. It's too scary.

I put my enclosed headphones back on once more, to flee from the world as it was swallowed into its ultimate doom, to attempt to detach myself from it all.

The radio was already cut off. All that remained now was static.

"...It's time to give it up. Everything..."

The moment I whispered it, I suddenly thought that I heard something.

Straining my ears, I found it was a voice. A voice speaking to me.

—Then, in a flash, I realized.

This was my voice. No one else's.

"Hey, can you hear me? There's something you still have to do before going...Something you have to tell him, right?"

I couldn't remember what it was.

But, for whatever reason, I felt like I understood the meaning behind the warning.

"It'll be okay. Trust me. If you can get over that hill, you'll know what I'm talking about, whether you want to or not. If you stay where you are, you're gonna disappear. Hey—"

I wiped away the tears threatening to run down my face once more, then took a deep breath.

"—You want to survive, don't you?"

It was the day the earth came to an end.
I planted my foot down upon the undulating ground as hard as I could, just as my voice guided me to.

YUUKEI YESTERDAY I

The piercing sound of the alarm woke me up.

I craned a hand to the side, searching for the source of the noise, before grabbing my cell phone by the cord.

Then I shut off the alarm, checked the time, and with a heavy sigh, closed my eyes once more.

...Hang on. This is weird. Like, really, really weird.

According to the clock, I had slept for eleven whole hours today.

So why am I so deathly tired? This is *such* a rip-off. This high-school teenager, at the peak of her flowering, has just given up the entirety of her late night—a costly loss indeed—and yet the relief this had granted her body was downright paltry.

What could have gone wrong? Am I not as flowery as I've led myself to believe? Maybe there wasn't much I did while awake besides play online games, but the price I had paid for this sleep was dear, too dear.

A sense of malaise settled over my body, sending frantic danger signals: "Stop! Think it over! If you don't sleep some more, you're gonna die!"

My brain, upon receiving this distress call, sprang into action, considering all methods available to avoid getting up out of the futon.

For example, Plan A: Fake Sickness.

Right now, I live alone with my grandmother. If I just told her something like "Ooh, I'm not feeling too well today...," it'd be a cinch to take the day off from school.

Tricking my grandmother wouldn't win me any brownie points, no, but there wasn't much to be done about it. Desperate times call for desperate measures.

*   *   *

But this strategy possessed some critical flaws.

If I went too far with complaining about feeling sick, my grandmother might whisk me away to the hospital.

I'd be subject to examination, maybe even admitted...and just thinking about the concept made my heart plunge into my stomach.

Lying in some hospital room, no video games, nothing to help pass the time at all? Not gonna happen.

Besides, people are way too edgy about this sort of thing anyway. An "illness" like the one I have is hardly any matter of life and death. But some people just go nuts over anything.

My dead grandfather, in particular. He was always on pins and needles about my illness, going through all these hoops and going way overboard for my sake—enough so to make the high school I was admitted to this year treat me like some kind of tumor.

...Of course, from other people's perspectives, I suppose my habit of suddenly fainting right away in the middle of class *is* a tad irritating. That, and embarrassing to me.

"You know, if you think about all of that, things are probably best right now as they are."

—It's been six or so months since I started living under that credo. That might be one of the reasons why I have yet to make any kind of decent friends.

Be that as it may, Plan A was a nonstarter.

Contemplating the issue and reaching this conclusion took approximately two minutes. Factoring in the Law of Real Time Versus Relative Time Experienced While In Bed, this speed had to be worthy of praise.

Plan B: I Actually Have Off School Today.

If I told my grandmother that today was an optional day or something...But then I remembered that she asked me, "Did you need a bento lunch tomorrow?" last night and I replied, "Yeah! Couldja make up some fried eggs?"

...I am so *stupid!* Why fried *eggs,* of all things?! I didn't need any bento—I should have requested a sleep-time extension ticket. Not that that exists or anything.

As if to defy this thought, the inviting smell of eggs cooking over a burner wafted into the room. Chef Grandma must have been cooking my bento right now, giving everything she could to fulfill my request.

"Nnnngh," I muttered, full of guilt over expending all this effort to come up with an excuse to goof off. Could I possibly be any less considerate of my poor old grandmother?

Rolling over, I burrowed my way back underneath the covers and pushed the reset button on my mind.

...How can my grandmother even *do* that, anyway? The way she always wakes up at the crack of dawn, day in and day out, no alarm required? The only answer I had was that she had some kind of precision stopwatch installed in her body. My grandma's a cyborg...

—As my brain stumbled its way from one inane thought to the next, I heard the creaking and whining of someone climbing up the stairs. The creaking was straight out of horror movies, the kind you only hear in old wooden houses, and it probably—no, *definitely* meant that I was about to be forced out of the futon.

I tugged the sheets tighter over my body, making one final, noble struggle.

Ughh...I'm out of time...Plan C...Plan C...Plan—

"You gonna be in there all day or what?! Hurry up and get dressed before you wind up late!"

"Ergh...yeah..."

Mission failed.

Blazing sunlight poured through the opened curtains. GAME OVER flashed in red lettering across my mind.

*

A balmy late-autumn morning.

The haze-laden dog days of summer were behind us. Most of the fall was too, making my surroundings on the journey to school seem positively wintry by now. You could notice the extra layers beginning to appear on the bodies of other students. A few couples passed by in sweaters as they got friendly with each other.

—I flashed obvious glares of animosity at these students, shutting out their asinine conversations with my headphones as I silently plodded toward school. I, Takane Enomoto, was in an *extremely* bad mood.

Although maybe this isn't even worth noting. To me, this is the default.

Since I had grown accustomed to staying up late, I was generally tired and crabby throughout the prenoon hours, from the moment I opened my eyes in the morning.

Perhaps due to that, my facial expression had grown into one of plain and apparent malice. People asked me if I was angry over something all the time.

And that, of course, would only make me crabbier. It was a seriously vicious cycle.

I wouldn't mind more of a carefree life, giggling mindlessly at things and engaging in wacky teenage hijinks and so forth, but I never thought for a moment I could become that sort of girl, and I didn't want to anyway.

Even the delusions my mind conjured up about the ridiculous things I *could* become in the future annoyed me. Thus, I walked to school, just as peeved as any other day of my life.

*   *   *

My only salvation is that it's a fairly short way to school, one that doesn't require a bus or train to speed up.

That saves me from depleting my strength on the trip to school, and it also lets me sleep until the very last minute.

Thanks to that, I had leisurely pulled myself out of bed while the rest of the student body were struggling to catch their train connections. I was on track to reach the school gates a good fifteen minutes before homeroom.

Once I reached the road leading straight to my school, I spotted a sudden increase in the number of students wearing the same uniform I had on.

My walking pace instinctively accelerated, and my eyes grew more menacing than ever.

Removing my headphones just before the front gate, I rolled my coat up and placed it in my backpack.

I really liked these headphones. They were a birthday gift from my grandmother. They had kind of a cute design, and the sound quality was nice. I say "nice" just because the earbuds I borrowed from my classmates seemed kind of tinny by comparison; it's not like these were meant for rich audiophiles or anything.

But now that I was used to them, they had become my inseparable partner in life.

Giving a polite bow to the square-jawed gym teacher standing in front of the gate, I went inside to find the school grounds brimming with activity. All over, students were preparing for the school festival coming up in a week's time.

The spread-out path between the gate and the front entrance, several dozen meters in width, was dotted here and there with the booths allotted to each class for their festival activities.

I spotted several posters taped over some of them, from warnings

like WET PAINT! DO NOT TOUCH!! to requests like WE NEED CARD-
BOARD! IF YOU HAVE ANY, CONTACT THE 2-A CLASS PRESIDENT!

Looking around, I spotted students everywhere—one who must
have been working since dawn, what with all the paint spatters on
his clothing; one who was already dressed up like some kind of
movie monster; a girl whining about how "the guys in class never
do *anything* for us"; the classic "rah rah, this school festival is *sooo*
important, we gotta do our best!" kind of woman. It was all the
splendors of boundless youth, writ large before my eyes.

—But to someone like me, the classic "You spent all week making
snide remarks about me, and now all of a sudden you're acting like
my friend? What's with *that?*" kind of woman, all this festival prep
was nothing but one giant obstacle on the way to class.

The carnival atmosphere of the festival prep outside had revved
up the noise and energy inside school as well. Some of the students
had even stayed overnight, fooling around with each other in the
most despicable ways until dawn. It was deplorable.

And once all of this was over, the only thing the festival left behind
was an unfathomable amount of garbage.

What is *with* this pointless show? It's so stupid. Brainless.

And come to think of it, the printout handed out to Year 1, class B
yesterday, the class I'm (ostensibly) part of, mentioned that they'd be
doing perhaps the most hackneyed festival booth of them all—the
"maid café" route.

This kind of booth was something that I—who hardly attended
my officially assigned class at all, much less the festival-planning
conferences—was wholly unrelated to, a fact that I relished.

If I let myself get caught up in some crazy whim and actually
dressed up as a maid, it'd be a blemish I'd never be able to wipe away
for the rest of my life. Who could even *do* something like that to
themselves?

As I dwelled upon this nasty state of business, I glared hard enough at a dopey-faced boy blocking the way ahead, standing between the legs of a giant dinosaur model, to make him scurry aside as I headed for the front door.

Pushing a handle whose PUSH engraving had long disintegrated from overuse, I set foot inside the building, noticing that the heater was making the indoor temperature remarkably pleasant.

Removing my outside shoes, I turned an eye toward my shoe locker in order to fetch my indoor slippers. The wooden shelves were pretty ancient.

I had heard that the school building itself had a fair amount of history to it, a prestigious place of higher learning that birthed a wide variety of politicians, celebrities, and other famous people.

But, to be frank, most of the students would sooner talk about how much they hoped the school building would receive a sorely needed renovation before they boasted about its illustrious past.

During the typhoon that passed by this summer, our beloved alma mater had its gymnasium roof poked full of holes, the floor around the drinking fountain collapse within itself, and a whole variety of other pitiful disasters happen to it.

The most serious issue, though, came when the entire building's air conditioner blew itself up on the hottest summer day of the year. It was enough to make the majority of students eagerly hope for a school transfer.

Still, thanks to the bare minimum of repairs the school shelled out for during summer break, the HVAC system was back online. A portion of the student body, hoping to use the breakdown as a tool to earn themselves an extended summer vacation, were forced to reluctantly trudge back to school for the second semester.

Changing into my slippers atop the wooden grating by the front entrance, I briskly made my way down the hall.

This was the one moment in school life that always grieved me the most. Right where everyone turned left from the corridor with the shoe lockers, happily chattering amongst each other as they went upstairs to their normal classrooms, I alone turned right, heading for the labs and other subject-specific classrooms—in particular, a room with a distinctly chemical odor to it.

Yes. That's right. The "normal classroom" I reported to every day, thanks to the efforts of my assigned proctor, was the science storage room.

Due to the rapid influx of new students into the local neighborhood over the past few years, all the nonspecialized classrooms had already been assigned to groups of students, which meant that there were no classrooms left for the "special" classes to use.

In terms of equipment, any room would do as long as it had desks and a teacher's chair, but I still wished they gave at least a little more thought to my situation. I mean, I'm spending the majority of my three years as a high schooler, a teenager in full flower, inside a room that always faintly smelled of formaldehyde.

The thought would be enough to make anyone mope a bit, but since there were only two students (counting myself) assigned to this "classroom," it was a joy to spend time there in terms of serene quietude. Considering my illness, and considering how much of a persona non grata I'd be if I went back to a normal classroom at this point, I found it difficult to complain about this state of affairs.

Proceeding down the hall, I checked around me to ensure no one was near, then let out a long, dramatic sigh.

I passed by the art room, the music room, the home-ec room, before reaching the SCIENCE STORAGE plate on the right side of a broad, left-curving corridor leading to the club-activity rooms.

—Below the plate was a faded green sliding door I was all too familiar with.

I may have my complaints, but there was something oddly soothing about a classroom with only a few people inside.

My teacher was undoubtedly going to be late as always, and my sole classmate was the epitome of easygoing, spending the whole day drawing those pictures of his.

I opened the door, contemplating a quick nap before my teacher showed up, only to have a sight thrust before me that instantly dissipated any sleepiness I still had.

"Good morn...Aaaaggghhh!!"
"Huh? Oh, hey, Takane. Morning!"

There stood my sole classmate, Haruka Kokonose, not a single speck of malice lurking behind his broad smile.

His skin was a sickly pale of white, his bearing unfussy and unpretentious. His sole hobby was drawing, as was his sole talent. That kind of background (along with the name) seems remarkably womanly, but he was just a regular guy.

Except there was nothing "regular" about him right now.

—No matter which way you sliced it...he had nothing on apart from his boxers.

"W...wha...?!"
I was rendered speechless at this otherworldly turn of affairs so early in the morning. I tried to focus my eyes on something else, but he briskly walked straight toward me, as near-naked as before.

"Hey, uh, I can explain this...Earlier, over on the school grounds, there was this cat, right? And it kinda made a beeline for me, so I figured I'd pet it, but...like, it kept trying to dodge me and stuff, right? So then I lost my balance and fell into the fountain, so—"

"That's *fine*, that's fine!! I don't care why, okay?! Just...just put some clothes on!!"

My fervent shouting stopped Haruka in his tracks as he attempted to tell the tale behind his nudist habits, an "oh, woe is me" expression on his face. He tilted his head quizzically at me.

"Aw, come on. They aren't even dry yet. You see?"

He pointed at the school uniform drying in front of the heater, gesturing as if I was the one at fault here. He couldn't have been more than fifty centimeters away from me.

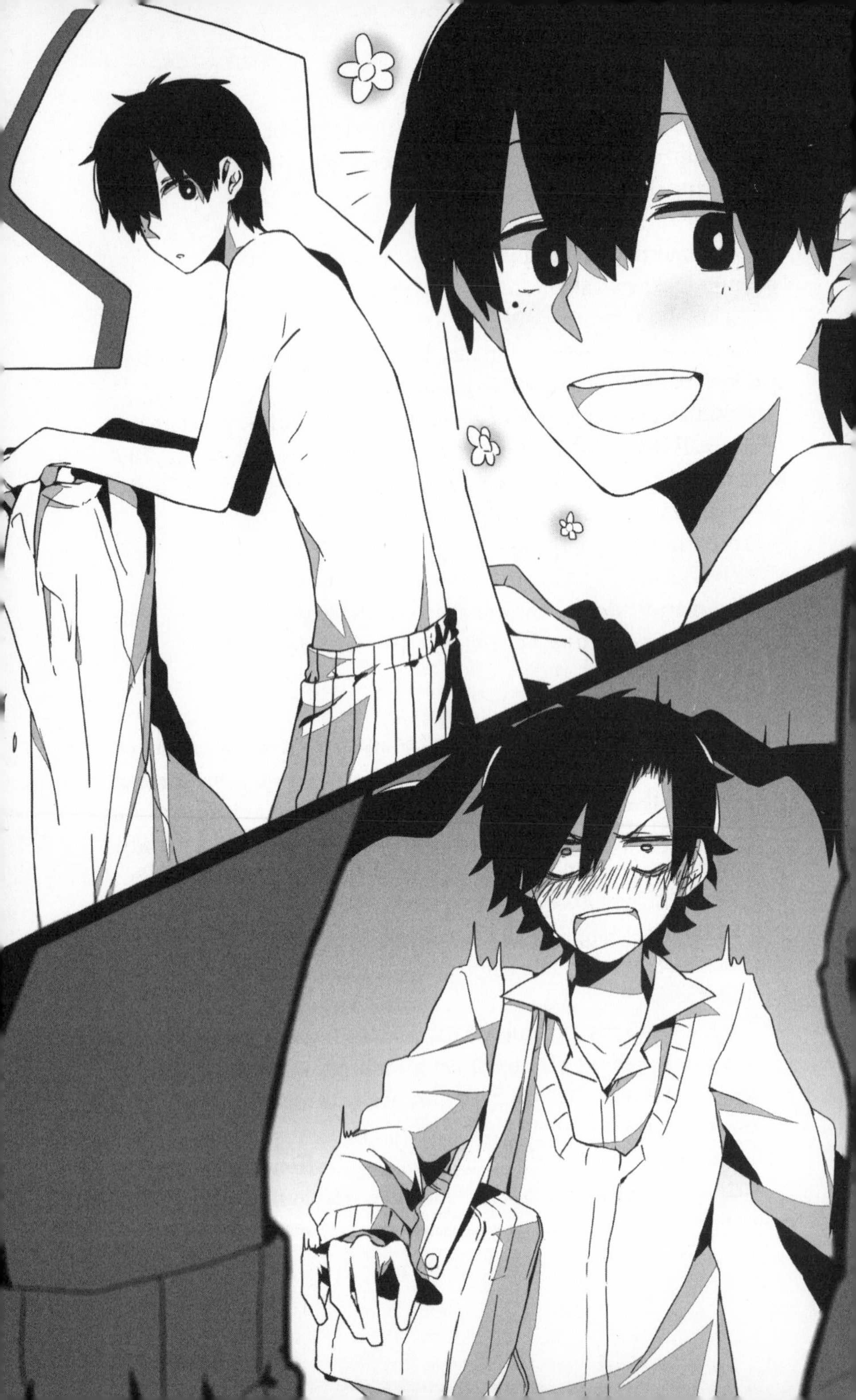

I reared back, unable to cope with this bizarre state of affairs, and tried my best to speak up for myself as my body banged against the sliding door I just closed.

"Ah…okay, okay! All right! It doesn't matter if it's wet or not! Just put that stuff on! I'll go find a jersey for you, so just put on everything else!!"

"Really? Well, okaaay…but, uhmm…hang on, where's my shirt? Shirt, shirt…"

"You're stepping on it, Haruka! Look down!…Ugh, just give it to me!"

With all the speed of an elderly tortoise, Haruka began to clothe himself, apparently incapable of grasping the full import behind this "half-nude in front of a girl" situation.

But I was in no shape to stand there and take it all in.

Grabbing the shirt Haruka picked up, I closed my eyes, trying to avoid the sight of him as I all but forced him to put it on.

"Whoa! Hey, I'm fine, I can put it on myself! Hey, that's the wrong sleeve…!"

"Aghh! Quit moving around! Don't point yourself this way!!"

No matter how you looked at it, this was *not* how normal people interacted with each other. Why do I have to force my only classmate to put his clothes back on, in school, first thing in the morning?

If this guy hadn't been the only other person in my class, I'd have no regrets turning him over to the police.

But if someone happened to see us right now, it'd be an utter disaster.

Who knows what kind of crazy *shoujo* manga-style misunderstandings this might lead to…? As I pondered over this, the absolute worst situation I envisioned came to life.

"Hey-yo! Time to get started with homeroom…uh?"

The leisurely voice chimed in as the door suddenly rattled open. On the other side stood our proctor, Kenjirou Tateyama, the teacher in charge of science classes at this school.

Tateyama's dumbfounded face likely provided a nice accompaniment to mine as his attendance record fell down to the floor.

"Oh…uh…So, Mr. Tateyama, this isn't what it…"

"Oh, mornin', Mr. Tateyama!"

In stark contrast to the way I was frozen in place, the nearly bare Haruka greeted our proctor with a broad smile.

From an impartial perspective, I imagine there was only one interpretation for this. Here was this meek, naive male student, and here was this evil-looking girl attempting to rip all the clothes off him.

I imagine the moment lasted for only an instant, but the silence that followed felt like an eternity to me. Mr. Tateyama, apparently coming to some sort of internal conclusion in his mind, said, "Oh… sorry if I, uh, intruded…" and attempted to make his way back to the hallway.

"Ahhhhh!! No! No, teacher! He was…he was going around without any clothes on, so I-I-I was just trying to help him get dressed!!"

Mr. Tateyama, his face conflicted as he tried to leave the classroom, suddenly stopped.

"Huh? Oh. Uh…okay, I get it. I just thought, you know, you guys couldn't restrain yourselves any longer or something…"

With a visible sigh of relief, our teacher flashed a smile at us as he picked the attendance ledger up off the floor.

"Could you stop acting like we're trying to go at each other all the time like that, sir? I mean, if we were, that'd be really bad news, wouldn't it?! You were trying to run away from us right now!"

"Yeahhh, well, you know, if something freaky's going on, it's always easiest if you pretend you were oblivious to it, right? You know what I mean…I just want you guys to grow and mature in as free an environment as I can give you, so…"

"Ugh, come *on!* That's totally awful, Mr. Tateyama! Can you at least help me get some clothes on this freak? I'm gonna call the administrator!"

Mr. Tateyama scratched his head in distracted reluctance, but the moment I mentioned the administrator, he whispered, "Okay," and with suddenly lightning-fast reflexes, he began to clothe Haruka.

As far as grown-ups go, you couldn't ask for much worse of a role model.

For a fleeting moment, I reflected about how, in his own way, Mr. Tateyama has given me a master class in what to avoid becoming when I'm older.

"Ergh...This is still all wet and clammy, sir..."

Haruka, once again decent thanks to Mr. Tateyama's nimble fingers, sounded utterly disgusted as he settled into his seat.

I sat down as well, but the moment my rear end touched the chair, I felt a sudden influx of extreme fatigue.

Who knows how many hit points I've already had to expend thanks to this idiot next to me?

Somehow I doubted I'd be smiling much for the rest of the day...

The teacher's desk was directly across from and slightly above the two student stations, neatly arranged next to each other. Mr. Tateyama settled into the high-backed folding chair behind his desk as he opened his attendance record.

"All right, Haruka, all right. I'll go find you a jersey later on...Uh, so anyway, good morning. Guess you're both in attendance, so... check, and check. Gotta say, I'm glad you guys haven't gotten bored of showing up here every day."

"That's...not really something a teacher should be saying, sir."

With a heavy thud, Mr. Tateyama placed his head on the desk. "Well, I'm the teacher, aren't I?" he whimpered. "So there you go, okay?"

There must be some kind of chronic staff shortage if someone like this guy is allowed to be with students.

It honestly gives me pause when I think about the future of this country.

"Oh, yeah, so homeroom this morning...Uh, what was it...? I'm pretty sure I made a note of it...unless I didn't..."

"Just tell us, sir!"

I was already irritated at the morning's events, but just looking at my teacher was enough to make the negative emotions within me swell to bursting. Watching him doodle in small circles in his ledger with a red pen reminded me of a bored grade-schooler staring into space during math class.

"Hang on, hang on…uh…Oh! That's right. We gotta come up with some kinda booth for the school festival soon, or else. What're you guys gonna do?"

"Whaa?! Didn't you say, like, 'Oh, who says you had to do anything?' the last time we asked about that, Mr. Tateyama?! We haven't thought about anything! We never even *talked* about it since then!"

I bolted out of my chair, pushing it back as I did, but Mr. Tateyama just stared at me with his zombielike eyes, unwilling to drum up the energy to stand himself.

"Well, yeahhhh, but…You know, last week, the administrator asked me what kind of booth my class was working on and stuff, so. I hadn't thought about anything, of course, so I just said to him 'Oh, we're working on a special surprise that'll knock your socks off, so watch out!'"

"Geez, Mr. Tateyama, how much do you want to suck up to the administrator, anyway?! Don't say we'll 'knock their socks off'! What're we gonna do?! There's only a week left…!"

I slumped back into my chair and covered my face with my hands. Next to me, I heard Haruka say, "Oooh, I'd kinda like to run a shooting gallery"—a silly idea he tossed out without any consideration of supplies or budgets. It only served to fan the flames of despair within me.

Honestly, I didn't care one bit about this teacher. But if this "special surprise" we were allegedly working on (not that we had any plans yet) wound up being advertised as such in the flyers passed around school, we were completely screwed.

Once that happened, all that awaited us was despair, darkness, and my final fall into the abyss of destruction…

"Errrggghh…!"

I couldn't help but groan out loud as I contemplated a future too nauseating to imagine. If I had any sort of capable classmates, maybe this sort of adverse challenge would've pushed all of us to passionate creativity, but having this drenched dunderhead next to me and one of the most despicably lazy teachers in the universe in front of us, we were distinctly lacking in war power.

Surely there was some kind of attack plan I could work on by myself...or so I thought. But thanks to my day-and-night gaming habit, or perhaps because I still hadn't fully woken up, my brain wasn't performing up to the standard I was hoping for.

I rubbed my head, trying to come to grips with the cruel reality thrust upon me and the utterly hopeless hand I had to offer in response, when I noticed Mr. Tateyama staring awkwardly at me.

"Uh...well, let's just calm down, okay? You're not gonna die or anything. We're free to use this classroom any way we want, more or less, and I'll be happy to help you guys out however I can. So could you just try to come up with something for me?"

Whatever confidence remained was crushed when our teacher (if I could even will myself to call him "teacher" any longer) added "I'll be happy to help you" to his feeble stab at a pep rally.

I wasn't remotely naive enough to have any faith in that.

If we came up with some lame plan for the festival despite the "special surprise" ad copy, I knew that'd result in rumors. Bad ones. I'd probably be unable to function for my remaining two years as a student here.

I doubt the thought even occurred in Haruka's mind, of course, but to me, this was nothing short of a crisis.

I was already persona non grata around school to some extent. Doing anything that'd make me stick out any further was something I had to avoid at all costs.

But I realized that Mr. Tateyama's offer to use this classroom as we wished opened up the slight possibility of a great breakthrough— some way out of this mess.

This room had grown to seem all but normal to the three of us, but for the casual visitor, it was packed with rare and unusual curios. If we put up displays touting "Experiment X" or whatever with the scientific stuff lying around, that'd no doubt get people excited.

"Well, gee, I hope we can come up with something interesting... Oh, but what about our budget? Each class gets a budget for their festival activities, right, Mr. Tateyama? How much can we get?"

The moment I asked the question, Mr. Tateyama's face froze—I could almost hear him nervously swallow—and he turned his eyes toward the equipment shelf behind us.

"Huh? What're you looking at—"

The gaze didn't escape my attention. I turned toward where I thought his eyes were pointed, only to find a bizarre, eerie-looking, yet oddly familiar fish specimen lying among the scientific equipment and bottles of chemicals.

It was a rare ocean specimen, one I had noticed Mr. Tateyama staring at as he glossed through an educational-materials website, muttering, "This specimen's so cool...but, ooh, it's pretty expensive..." to himself.

"Hmm? Hey, what's that? Didn't you say that specimen was too expensive, Mr. Tateyama?"

It was relatively chilly in the classroom, but I could see a small forest of sweat beads form upon Mr. Tateyama's forehead. He was unable to look me in the eye as I whipped out my trademark glare. He drooped downward silently, like a criminal in a detective manga just confronted with some kind of incontrovertible evidence, all but ready to reveal his motives and methods to the entire room.

"Mr. Tateyama, did...did you use up our festival budget?!"

"It...it's all *that* thing's fault...!"

He then went into an impassioned, unconvincingly acted defense of his crimes, which can be summarized as follows: Just as the budgets assigned to each class were being calculated, the rare specimen (i.e. "*that* thing") went on sale for 40 percent off. If he was expecting us to understand his motives, he did so in vain.

...That isn't even a real motive in the first place.

Watching him defend himself, as if *he* were the victim and the fish specimen was the real culprit, my emotions sped far beyond anger and revolution, eventually settling into something resembling sympathy.

"So, like, what're we gonna do? I mean...I still like the idea of a shooting gallery, but..."

As our teacher shifted gears to explain how charming and attractive the fish specimen was, and as I thought over how to best confront the administrator about this, Haruka parroted his shooting-gallery request once again, doggedly sticking to the only idea he was capable of conceiving.

"...If we do that, we'd need to have a lot of prizes to give out. It'd be a huge pain to prep. How could we pull that off with just the three of us? Plus, thanks to our stupid teacher, we don't even have any money to work with."

"Hmmm...I dunno, I thought it was a good idea, is all. I checked out what all the other classes were working on, and I don't think any of them were working on a shooting gallery, so..."

Haruka's tone was matter-of-fact, but it honestly seemed like a surprise to me. If no one else had a shooting gallery in the works, their budgets had to have something to do with it. With all the renovation issues the school's had to deal with, it's hard to imagine the administration gave enough of a budget to any class for a presentation that required fancy prizes to pull off.

But an even more pressing issue was Haruka here. Haruka, who usually just sat there glassy-eyed, making it impossible to guess what he was thinking, apparently was interested enough in the school festival that he knew what all of the other classes' presentations were going to be.

"...Huh. You must be looking forward to the festival an awful lot."

"Kind of," he replied, a little embarrassed. He didn't act that way at all back when he was in his skivvies in front of me. His standards for feeling shame must diverge a bit from the average person.

"That's kind of surprising. I mean, like, when we thought we weren't gonna do anything, you kept your mouth shut, so..."

"Yeah, but, you know, I'm not very strong, and it'd be a big deal if I suddenly collapsed or something. Prepping a booth looked really hard when I was looking at all of them, so I thought, you know...oh, well, right?"

Haruka flashed a fleeting smile as he spoke.

I wasn't up on the details, but I knew that Haruka's "illness" was something far more dark and serious than anything I had.

Something so severe, in fact, that if he had some kind of attack or whatever, it could easily lead to death. That kind of thing.

Mr. Tateyama told me about that long after I joined this school, but thanks to Haruka's easygoing, simpleminded approach to life, it just didn't seem real, somehow.

Haruka, for his part, seemed aware of it, as if he'd had some bad times in the past.

Perhaps this entire experience of going to school and interacting with other people had been a trial for him, in a lot of ways. And I just didn't notice it.

"Yeah, fair enough. But you wanna do *something*, right?"

"...I think I do, yeah. But, you know, I don't wanna put a bunch of stuff on you, Takane..." Haruka still acted bashful as he spoke to me. I didn't quite follow why this was making him act all fluttery like that.

"...Well, I know our teacher doesn't really give a crap either way, but you don't have to put up with that, Haruka. Just try and do something, okay? If you screw it up, you can worry about it then."

"Sure, yeah, but I can't do anything all by myself...I haven't really done anything like this, either...I dunno if I can really *do* it, you know?"

Watching Haruka hem and haw to himself as he rolled an eraser around his desktop made me unreasonably angry somehow. I slammed both palms against my desk table.

"—Ugghhh!! Stop acting all wishy-washy like that!! You wanna run a shooting gallery, right? Well, great! Let's do it! I'll help you set it up! All *right?!*"

I fully exercised my latent talent for glaring as I shouted at Haruka. "All right..." he whispered, a look of abject fear on his face.

It wasn't enough to placate me. Turning back toward Mr. Tateyama, I continued my tirade.

"Mr. Tateyama, *please,* go withdraw some money for us! We're gonna give out that specimen as a prize, too, okay? *Okay?!*"

"Whaaa?! Wait, we…We don't have to go *that* far! How much do you think that cost—"

"…Administrator."

"Right! Roger that! Let's go with that idea! Boy, this is starting to get exciting, huh?"

Mr. Tateyama threw together the most elated, refreshed face he could muster. Even Haruka stared coldly at him, finally keying in to just how despicable our proctor really was.

—Looking at the clock, over half an hour had passed since homeroom began. We were already well into the first period of class.

In this school, classes were more or less shunted aside for the week before the school festival. Instead, the planning committee for each class took over, guiding the students as they prepped their festival presentations.

First period was held in the homeroom for every class, but after that, the students were likely sent off to the classrooms where their festival prep work awaited them.

The original idea was that Haruka and I would generally engage in self-study type stuff during this time, but since we were now tasked with coming up with a killer idea, we had to get to work. And fast.

"Still, I dunno…Target shooting and all…How should we, like, get started?"

I knew I had just all but overwhelmed Haruka into the choice a moment ago, but really, how much *could* the two of us do to set up a shooting gallery in a week's time?

We'd need to buy some prizes, for one, as well as build a stand to display all of them. That, and the cork pop-guns. The more we thought about it, the more the tasks piled up before us.

We'd need to use the art room and shop room to build the bigger props, but I figured that the classes who had planned a bit earlier than we did had already filled up all the available time slots.

"Uhm…If you think we can't do it, maybe we could do something else instead?"

"No! Forget it! It's only impossible if we *think* it is! You're the one who wanted to go through with it. Think of something!"

Haruka flinched again before crossing his arms together and nodding in agreement, eyes closed.

It *was* his idea…at first, anyway. But I was a driven girl, my mind racing with the thought of showing everyone else that we weren't like them, not like the others. Not all bubbly and ditzy and airheaded.

If we were gonna go through with this, I didn't want to do it half-cocked. My days and weeks of online gaming had forged in me a sense of high ambition, and now—for *this*, of all things—that ambition was starting to blaze.

"One thing's for sure, though—we can't really build any kind of big, fancy stand or anything. You aren't good at do-it-yourself stuff or anything, are you, Mr. Tateyama?"

"Nope! Never tried any of it!"

"—Yeah, I figured. Which means that you and I will have to do it ourselves, Haruka…"

"Whoa, whoa, hang on a sec! Okay, I'll admit I'm no handyman or anything, but, you know, I'm pretty good at programming and stuff!"

Mr. Tateyama pointed a thumb at himself, flashing that asinine "I'm really great at this one thing you'd *never* understand!" aura you see a lot from otaku nerds.

"Huh. Yeah, wow, neato. So, anyway, you'll just get in the way, so why don't you go code a dating simulator or—"

Dealing with him was starting to exasperate me. I was just trying to humor him, but somewhere along the line, I had inadvertently said what I was thinking out loud.

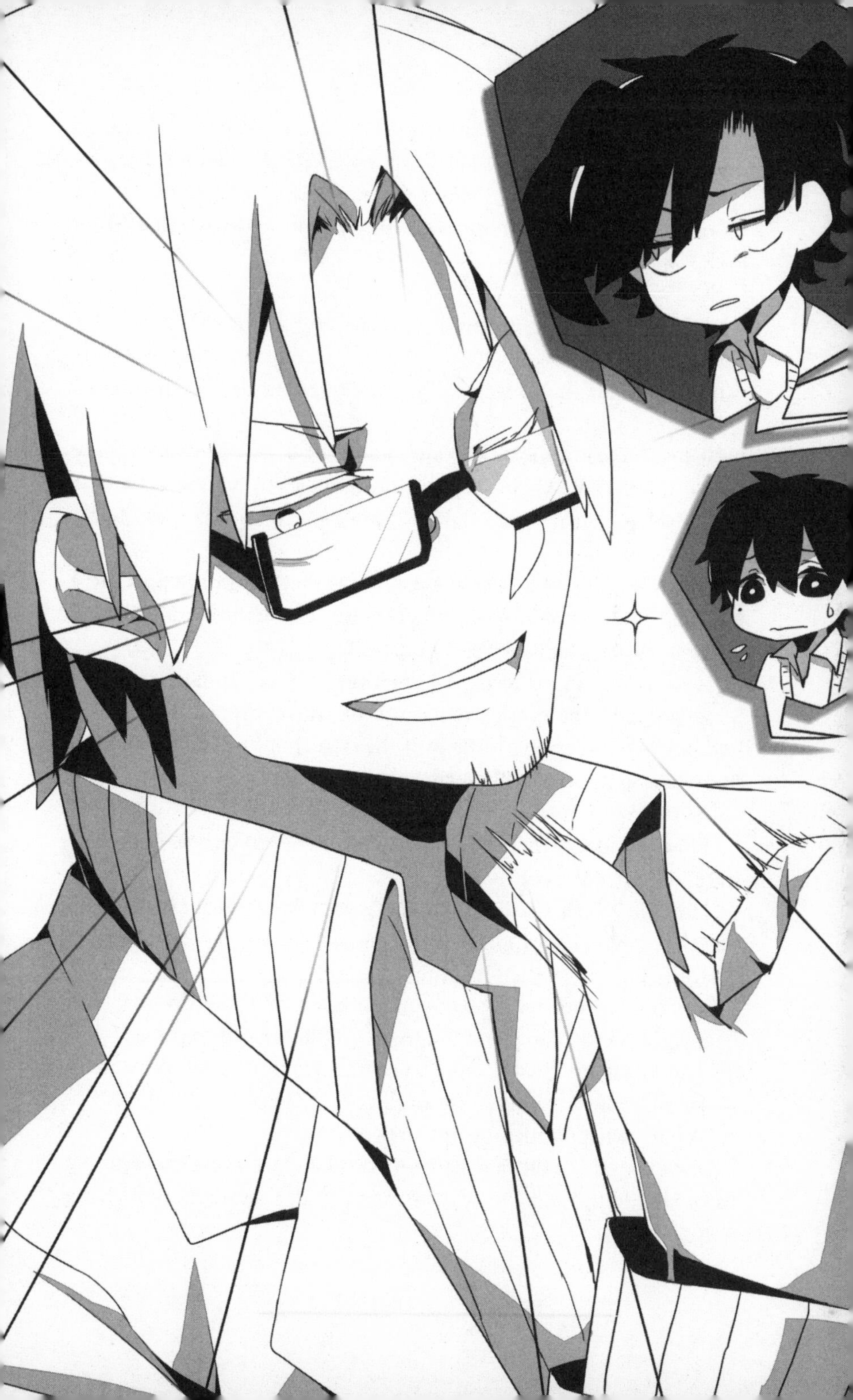

*   *   *

We were wholly incapable of fabricating anything large or elaborate.

The only prize we had to offer was a rare fish specimen.

Our goal: to create the most exciting shooting gallery that mankind ever saw.

It was a gamble, but maybe, just maybe, it was something we could fabricate within a week.

Before I knew what I was doing, my chair clattered backward as I stood up.

"Whoa, whoa, whoa! T-Takane, just wait a sec! Look, I'm sorry about all this, okay? So let's settle this peacefully! Violence isn't gonna solve anything, all right?! There's got to be some way to do this...!"

Mr. Tateyama, surprised at this abrupt motion on my part, held his hands in front of him, whimpering his response like an evil RPG minion doomed to die for story purposes.

As for Haruka next to me...I don't know if he had fallen sleep as he attempted to at least pretend to think things over or if all of this had pushed his gentle psyche over the edge, but he had fallen to the floor, taking the loudly clattering chair with him.

"I have an idea, Mr. Tateyama! I think we might be able to pull off the shooting gallery!"

"Uh? Oh. Yeah, that. But that's gonna be a huge pain to get together, right? I mean, like I told you earlier, I've never even successfully put a bookshelf together, so..."

"No, no, I'm not relying on you at all for anything on that. But, like, you said you can program, right? Right, Mr. Tateyama...?"

I smirked at my teacher. He blanched in response, plainly aware of where this conversation was going.

"What...what's with you, Takane?"

There was still a bit of spittle on Haruka's face as he spoke to me from behind the chair he was sitting behind. I decided not to bring it up.

"Hee-hee-hee…I was just saying that we might be able to do this shooting gallery after all. You're good at drawing, right…?"

"Eeeep…!"

I tried to smile as broadly as I could, but Haruka looked absolutely terrified, as if I was attempting to blackmail him. Why does every male (well, both of them) in this room have to be so pitiful?

But, really, it didn't matter how pitiful they were right now.

…After all, they just had to do as I told them, and everything would be fine.

"H-hang on, Takane…This 'shooting gallery' you're thinking of…"

Judging by his facial expression, Mr. Tateyama had likely already figured out what I was thinking.

It was understandable, given that his share of the work to make this "shooting gallery" happen was nothing short of massive.

"Hee-hee-hee…You guessed it. We don't need a table saw or anything to make a shooting gallery *game*, right? Haruka could draw the characters and backgrounds, and if we went with that, one prize would be all we need."

Once I finished, Mr. Tateyama's shoulders dropped, as if he was saying "Ahh, I knew it…" with his entire body.

A single person creating a video game all by himself would be a fairly massive amount of work.

But Mr. Tateyama had been lazing around, doing his own thing in the classroom for long enough. Considering that, he owed us that much labor by now, if not more.

"Huh…? We're gonna make a game? Starting now?!"

Even the normally placid Haruka seemed startled, a surprise given how hard it was to get him to react to anything. Unlike Mr. Tateyama, though, there was a palpable measure of excitement behind the response.

"Well, yeah! You can draw all of the graphics for the game, right? That'd be pretty exciting for you, I bet."

Haruka energetically nodded in response. His unbelievably bright expression, something unlike anything he usually wore, gave him a distinctly different impression than usual.

"Well, I know it's gonna be kinda tough, but hang in there, okay? Like, I'm sure Mr. Tateyama will figure something out in the end, so…"

"Whaa?! Why's it gotta be me?! Do you have any idea how much it takes to code a whole—"

"Administr…"

"I'll give it everything I've got! It's gonna be the best gallery you ever saw!!"

Mr. Tateyama gave us a thumbs-up, his face one of pure, unadorned affirmation.

This "administrator" magic word was proving surprisingly useful. There was no doubt that I'd be relying on it for the rest of my high-school career.

"But let me ask you something. What did you mean by 'one prize would be all we need'? There's no way we can predict how many people will beat the game, you know…And if we made the game so hard that nobody could beat it, that'd turn off people even more, wouldn't it?"

"Oh, you don't have to worry about that. Just have it so you're try-ing to score points instead of finishing the whole game. Also, make it two-player only, okay?"

"Sure, that wouldn't be any problem, but…you aren't talking about…"

"Exactly! I'll complete against anyone who shows up, and we'll play for the highest score. Playing against a girl like me, you aren't gonna get any complaints about the game's difficulty then, right?"

The blood had returned to Mr. Tateyama's face. Now his expres-sion was one of sheer exasperation, the exact same face I had given to him a moment ago. I reveled in it for a second.

"*You're* gonna play against everyone, Takane? But if you lose even once, we're gonna have to give up our prize, aren't we?"

"Yeah, assuming that ever happens. Who said I was ever gonna lose? I'll just lose on purpose right toward the end of the school festival, and we'll be the talk of the whole school. I'll make sure that it works out that way."

Listening to this, Haruka looked more and more anxious by the moment. I couldn't blame him.

No one can predict what would happen in a video game. There was always a non-zero chance of me losing at any time.

And if I did lose and we had to give up our single prize (Rare Fish Specimen [Extremely Expensive]), that essentially meant the end of our festival booth. A pretty ambitious bet, in other words.

But I possessed a certain "special ability," one I hadn't gotten around to revealing to these guys.

…Actually, I hoped I'd never have to tell anyone about it, but that ability was what gave me so much confidence that we'd win this bet. Not that I ever want to breathe a word of it to anybody, but—

"You know, Haruka, she might just do it, too. She's, like, a celebrity on the net. You know that game they keep showing ads for on TV? The one with the dude blowing away all those zombies?"

"Oh, yeah, I've seen that. One of those online games, right…? I think there was some kinda championship a bit ago…"

"Right, right. And Takane placed second in the nationals there."

Just as I was expanding upon my internal monologue to myself, my teacher, much to my abject surprise, tossed me out of the closet.

"Ahhhghghhh!! W-w-what're you talking about?! I-I'm not anything like…"

The name of the game was *Dead Bullet -1989-*, an online shooter where you mowed down wave after wave of zombies. It had attracted a vast swath of users since its launch a year or so ago, to the point where it was now one of the leading FPSes in the Japan market. I was kind of a veteran player, having made it to the top ranks approximately four hours after the game launched.

Thanks to the unique strategic approach I brought to the game, my name was famous enough that I boasted a fan community with several hundred members. But, thanks in part to the rather narrow channels of communication I retained with most people, my teacher was the only person in real life who knew about this. —Until now, that is.

It was a critical error in judgment. I was looking for someone I could share this game with in the real world, and since Mr. Tateyama demonstrated an ability to discuss even the finer details of *Dead Bullet* with me, I invited him into my community. Big mistake.

The thing about *Dead Bullet -1989-* is that it's a grotesquely violent title, one with an overwhelmingly male audience—not the kind of thing a teenage girl would flock to over all other forms of entertainment.

To be honest, it was the sort of game that, if one of the other female students got addicted to it, I'd be hesitant to come near her.

And now the truth's been revealed to my sole classmate…

"Wow, Takane! Second in the whole country? That's really surprising! Why didn't you tell me until now? Is it, like, really fun?"

But Haruka, completely unaware of my internal conflict, gave me a surprisingly favorable reaction, to the point where he acted like he wanted to know more.

No doubt that's because he didn't know what the game was all about. If he knew more about it, there's no doubt the reaction would be more like "LOOOOOLLLL look at this scary chick playing this freaky horror game…stay away from her!!!!" or something.

As I winced at Haruka's meek, questioning eyes, Mr. Tateyama suddenly let out a belly laugh as he revealed yet more horrifying secrets.

"There, you see, Takane? You were looking for friends to play with, weren't you? I'm not really all that good at *Dead Bullet*, so I thought, hey, why not invite Haruka?"

"Huhh?! W-what're you talking about?! It's not like I play it all that much or anything…"

Which was a lie. Because I did. I fell asleep early due to exhaustion yesterday, but generally, I threw myself into the world of the game from four p.m., when I got home from school, until four a.m. the next morning.

Mr. Tateyama, still guffawing in front of me, was fully aware.

"Oh, reeeeally? I figured you'd play it a lot more if you were that into it. I mean, what was your handle? Something like 'Dancing Flash'—"

"Agh! Nooooo!! Listen! I'm gonna call the administrator, okay?! I'll tell him *everything*! All right?!"

"Whoa whoa whoa whoa! Hey, don't joke about that sort of thing! I'm sorry, all right?!"

Someone watching the two of us jostle our desks around as we screamed at each other would undoubtedly find the whole scene quite hilarious.

But to us, this was a life-and-death battle.

The moment Haruka said, "Hey, uh, calm down..." as we glared at each other for several seconds, the school bell rang, as if to put a final end to our stalemate.

"...Oof. How 'bout we just agree to keep quiet, all right? About everything."

"Yes...That sounds like the best thing to me. But don't get me wrong, Mr. Tateyama. If you leak anything else about me..."

"And likewise for you, Takane. Breathe anything to the administrator, and you know what'll happen, right?"

"...Right. I follow you. I'll just bottle it up inside me...But I'm not gonna let you divulge anything else about me, okay?"

As my teacher and I attempted to stare each other into submission, exchanging a conversation that hardly seemed like a healthy educational exchange, the first-period homeroom class came to a close.

"Right...Well, I guess this is partly my fault, too. Guess I'll see what kinda stuff I can come up with, huh? ...So let's spend this next period working out the details, all right? Feel free to go to the bathroom if you want."

With that, Mr. Tateyama picked up the attendance ledger and left the classroom, index finger scratching his forehead. For just a moment, I could hear the footsteps and excited conversations from passing students from beyond the open door.

"Boy...You think we can really do this?"
Haruka made eye contact with me as I threw myself back into my desk chair, utterly drained.
"...You sure made a lot of promises, Takane, but I dunno...This is kinda really starting to get exciting, huh...? I think we can really do this! I'll do my best, okay?"
Watching Haruka give a fist-forward "We can do it!" pose after his little declaration made me suddenly feel like my face was burning a bright red. I could only assume it was out of embarrassment at having my illustrious online career revealed to the world.

—I let out a light smile.

Then I realized I had become what I hated the most—one of those "rah rah, this school festival is *sooo* important, we gotta do our best!" girls. My smile was no doubt borne from the sheer shame of it all, rather than coming from any actual happiness.

"...Well, at least we won't be bored."

As I muttered it to no one in particular, my mind was already beginning to formulate a schedule of tasks to handle before our boundlessly exciting school festival began.

HEADPHONE ACTOR II

I didn't think I'd seen the landscape before me transform so wildly as this ever before in my life.

With every step I took, another stoplight was sent flying, another building swayed wildly over its foundation.

The air shifted and swirled before me, and my body propelled itself forward through the wind with every breath I took.

The intersection was packed with people.

The signals and signs had already lost all meaning to them, and the lawless roads were now host to a gaggle of colorful cars, abandoned in assorted unlikely locations and angles.

Some people were screaming something or other.
Some were punching and flailing at their fellow man.

All of them looked petrified, wailing pitifully at the end of the world.

The screaming infant I heard for just a moment almost made me stop running.

"Keep going. This area's going to be all over within twelve minutes, so don't let yourself look back at them…Make a left at the next light."

The voice from my headphones, unlike the mad scene before my eyes, was calm and composed as it matter-of-factly provided navigation.

So I kept going, following its directions as I thrust myself forward through the waves of people.

I began to wonder how many times in my life I had truly ran with all my strength up to now.

I led a sheltered childhood from early on, enough so that I was never given a chance to roam free outside.

That was because I had an illness. One where I lose consciousness in a completely unpredictable manner. No reason, no warning.

This wasn't an illness that flared up all that often.

But the problem was, I could never recall the exact moment when I fell to the ground.

My memory clocked back into action from the point after I opened my eyes.

My recollection from before I blacked out would always be hazy and undefined, as if I was having a long, extended dream.

Cutting through the crowds, running through narrow alleys, I was ejected into a large, wide avenue.

"Turn right here! There's only one minute left..."

The voice inside my headphones had gradually taken on a sense of urgency.

Paying no attention to my aching legs, I immediately pivoted myself to the right, only to hear a sound like crumpling metal behind me.

I became unable to resist the urge to turn around as I heard the screams follow in succession.

"...Hurry! You have someone you need to see, right?! Please..."

My consciousness began to grow hazy as my breathing accelerated. I felt my lungs begin to burn.

I wonder if I'm going to black out again.

Come to think of it, when was the last time I lost consciousness?

...I grew unable to recall anything at all.

How did all of this even happen?

Who was I even trying to reach...?

*   *   *

And yet, I still felt like there was something extremely important waiting for me at the end.

That feeling was the only thing that pushed my legs forward.

—Turning forward, I saw the hill I had been running toward right in front of me.

YUUKEI YESTERDAY II

"Daaang…That girl's beat thirty-seven in a row…"

"Yeah, I heard from some guy that she actually placed second nationwide in a *Dead Bullet -1989-* tournament."

"Dude! Really?! You mean 'Dancing Flash Ene'?! Man, no wonder she's so dialed in like that. Whoa, check it out, she beat her high score again! …But why's she crying, though?"

The science storage room was undoubtedly witnessing the most exciting scene it had ever hosted since the school's opening.

I kept a firm grip on my controller, unable to wipe the tears away from my eyes.

No matter how hard things got, once I picked up the controller, there was nothing that could take my hands off of it.

That was the credo I lived by as a gamer, something that lay at the root of my personality, and I wasn't sure I could do anything to break the habit any longer.

The big-screen monitor displayed a hand holding a gun at the bottom, twisting left or right based on my controller input as it shot down the barrage of targets.

The target monsters that roared dramatically with every hit were drawn like cutesy fairy-tale bears and rabbits and so on, but the explosion of blood and body parts that gushed forth with every shot was not exactly kid stuff.

"Nice, Takane! Another win for us! …Though that was really more of an Ene move just now, wasn't it?!"

Haruka, all but serving as my ringside manager as he sat next to my competition seat, beamed brightly as his eyes shone in sheer wonder.

"Uh. Ngh. Shut…up…dumb…ass…"

I was already sobbing to the point where stringing together a sentence was proving difficult, but the audience surrounding us paid it no heed, showering me with applause as my win count continued to skyrocket upward.

My competitor, a guy dressed in military gear and a crew cut, gave me an impassioned salute. "I appreciate this," he said. "Such an honor! Getting to play against Dancing Flash Ene in person like this...!"

It was to the point where the brawny men milling around the entrance were scuffling against each other for the chance to challenge me next. "Let me go first," said one. "No! No, I'm more worthy of her!" said another.

The students who had gathered around to take in the scene, along with the hard-core gamers who heard the rumors and ran over for this once-in-a-lifetime chance, had turned the room into a living hell.

"Why is this happeninggggggg...?"

My vision blurred as the tears plopped down onto the controller.

*

The day of the school festival. The trigger for this whole ordeal began a few hours before.

The usual desks were carted out from the center of the science storage room, the shooting-gallery booth looming large in their place.

Though, really, the "booth" was little more than a pair of monitors on top of a long table, a cloth decorated with fluorescent paint draped over it. But turning off the lights and taping cardboard over the classroom windows left the room in total darkness except for the monitors and the faint glow of the paint.

It didn't seem like any kind of last-moment setup at all, in no small part thanks to Haruka's artistic talent.

"W-well, this is it, huh...? It's kind of like a dream, isn't it? Like, we actually *did* this...!"

"Yep. Turned out pretty well, didn't it? Great job, Haruka! Here, let me practice a little more before we open this up."

Mr. Tateyama, deep rings around his eyes after pulling a series of death-march all-nighters to finish coding the game, and myself, with no rings around the eyes at all after getting ample sleep (fifteen hours) the night before, were busy making the final adjustments before the big reveal.

Haruka turned on the PC lurking beneath the table, and in a few moments, the title screen for the game, the pride and joy of Haruka and Mr. Tateyama, appeared.

The game, which featured a rogues' gallery of plush animal monsters getting mown down by the player, was named *Headphone Actor* by Haruka.

I didn't know what the title was supposed to mean at first glance, until I found that the final boss, the evil mastermind controlling all these monsters, looked exactly like me. In other words, the object was to defeat the headphoned villain and the troupe of evil monsters ("actors") she had under her control. Then I knew what it meant, and it irritated me *more* than a tad.

It goes without saying that I floored Haruka with a single punch immediately afterward.

"...This is really in bad taste, you know that? Why do I have to fight against myself?"

"Well, I mean, the people who play this have to beat you in the game to win, right? So I figured, like, it'd be neat if the last boss looked kind of like you, Takane...though I guess I kinda forgot *you'd* be playing the whole time, too..."

"...I should've guessed it'd never occur to you. Though it doesn't look much like me anymore, now that you changed the colors."

The last boss, named "Takane V2" by Mr. Tateyama, used to be a dead ringer for me with her black hair. After I forced Haruka to change it, she was now in her "alternate Player 2 palette" with blue hair.

"But even ignoring that, why'd you make this game into such a gorefest? Did we really need *that?*"

Pressing the "Start" button on the title screen brought up an opening monologue. The game was apparently set in a small city, one that (once again due to Haruka's meandering artistic spirit, no doubt) bore an eerie resemblance to the town we lived in.

Proceeding through this townscape, gun in hand, the player is confronted with a gauntlet of cutesy stuffed animals, all eager to attack you. Your job is to shoot them down, but with every hit, the game rewarded you with blood spurts and grisly, moist sound effects, no doubt striking most players with intense pangs of guilt.

"That was...You know, I borrowed it from that game you were talking about before, Takane! I figured that's the kind of thing you'd like, so..."

My fingers quivered in response. That error in judgment was all it took for a stuffed monkey to sink its teeth into my neck, bringing the game to a quick end.

Streams of blood poured down from the top of the screen, followed by GAME OVER in block lettering.

"D-did you hear about that from Mr. Tateyama?!"

After several nights without sleep, Mr. Tateyama had apparently collapsed into bed after finishing up the game, leaving behind the words "Tell...the administrator...about this..."

Haruka had apparently been staying over at our teacher's house over the past week to get the game done. There was more than a passing chance Haruka had learned a lot more than he should have.

"No, no, he didn't tell me anything. I just remembered what you told me in class earlier, and I did some research from there."

"Oh! Well, that's fine then, but...I mean, don't you think all this blood is kind of a mismatch for the theme of the game? It kind of, I dunno, puts a damper on things."

I started the game from the beginning again, but the sight of these cutesy plush animals getting gibbed with every shot just felt weird to me. If these were zombies, the whole package would've been a lot more attractive, I thought.

"Heh-heh! Sorry about that. But, hey, it's the school festival, so I wanted to make it something you'd like..."

My hands slipped once again at this most uninvited of responses. This time, a plush pig trampled me to death for a quick GAME OVER.

"But...it's not like I, like, *enjoy* all this gore or anything..."

I deliberately kept my gaze away from Haruka as I started another game.

"What? Ooh...uh, I'm sorry. I thought you liked this kind of rough stuff, so...But I guess you wouldn't after all, huh, Takane? Guess I should've realized that sooner."

"Oof...Man, you *really* got the wrong idea with me, Haruka. Listen, do you know what makes for a good game? Excitement. You play a game because it's fun and refreshing to be the hero, going around this amazing world and wishing you were more a part of it."

That was the attraction I looked for in games, at least.

The real world could be a lot more unfair, but in the game world, if you have the talent, anyone can be a hero.

That, more than anything else, was why I became a gamer.

"Hohh...I see. I don't really play games much, so I guess I wasn't aware. So, uh, does that mean this game...isn't very fun or whatever?"

Haruka sounded cautious as he asked. I kept my eyes firmly on the screen, saying, "Oh, no, I kind of like it" after planting a shot between the eyes of a plush cat that flew into sight.

I could hear a sigh of relief from my side.

Given how much I already played the game yesterday, it only took ten minutes or so for me to get back into the groove.

Unless Haruka threw me with his unwelcome commentary and ended my game early, I never made a mistake. There was no way I could lose in a competitive match against another player.

One reason for this confidence was that I had easily tripled Mr. Tateyama's high score of 45,000 with my first play—a score he had to work hard to achieve.

"Wow, this is going to turn out great! No way could any of the challengers *here* beat you!"

"Well, duh. I've got the skills, and I know it, too...Whoa, look at what time it is! The festival's gonna start in five minutes! Are we okay with the rest of the prep, Haruka?!"

"Oh, uh, yeah, all systems go! I set everything up yesterday so we'd be ready to go whenever. Ooh, but now I'm starting to get nervous..."

Haruka had been his usual "yeah, whatever" self up to now. Now, with the school festival looming large, the pressure must have been getting to him. He got out of his seat, pacing around the classroom anxiously.

"Hey! Quit freaking out on me! I'm not gonna lose to anyone, so it's gonna be just fine!"

"Y...yeah, I know, but you think anyone's gonna show up...? What if they don't like the game at all...?"

I, too, had begun to get butterflies in my stomach. It was the same kind of nervousness, I recalled, that I felt before the game tournament I went to the other day.

This time, though, the main challenge wasn't to see how well I could perform—it was how much I could entertain the guests that showed up.

We'd be entertaining everyone from kids to elderly women...Of course, we'd have to put in some age restrictions with all this gore, but either way, we'd be obliged to appeal to a broad audience.

The game Mr. Tateyama and Haruka came up with was naturally pretty lacking in terms of gameplay depth and balance, but to be honest, I thought it was pretty fun. There was something really compelling to it that made you want to keep playing.

My job was to bring this appeal across to the audience, helping them enjoy it as much as possible...and try to keep a smile on my face the whole time.

"Aw, don't worry about it. You put your heart and soul into this, right? They're gonna love it!"

I tried my best to placate the fretful Haruka. Just as I did, the speaker next to the clock squawked to life: "Ladies and gentlemen, the school festival is about to begin. All classes, follow your planning committee's instructions and make this into the most exciting event you can!"

The moment the voice fell quiet, my heartbeat accelerated.

Haruka, for his part, was crouched down, intoning "It'll be okay, it'll be okay" to himself like a mantra.

"Hey! Get up! We're starting! People are gonna start coming in soon, so...uh, go stand in front of the door and guide them in! If anyone looks interested, go up to them and tell them what's going on in here! Okay?!"

"Uh, uh, yeahhh…Yeah! I…okay. It'll be okay, it'll be okay…"

With that less-than-inspiring reply, Haruka stood up and staggered his way toward the door…and right into it, with a bang. "Ow, ow, ow…" he said as he finally exited the classroom.

"…You think he's gonna be okay?"

The speaker that had just played the announcement was now broadcasting background music for the festival, letting everyone know that things were about to get under way.

For the purposes of our setup, I turned down the volume on the science storage room's speaker, shut off the lights, and decided to wait for Haruka to presumably bring in my first challenger.

With the lights out, the room was bathed in the faint light from the monitors and the fluorescent paint.

I sat down on the rightmost of the two chairs facing the monitors on the long table, staring blankly at my title screen.

The *Headphone Actor* splash screen featured a dull, gray cityscape behind the title logo. The game must have been set around dusk, because a deep, purplish sky was visible through the tops of the buildings.

"Man, this game is *really* in bad taste…I mean, Haruka and Mr. Tateyama really got into making it and all, but this is gonna freak you out if you're a girl or something, isn't it?"

But I knew Haruka. I doubted he cared. If he found an interested-looking girl, I was sure he'd take her right into the room, like I told him to.

—You know, this could actually turn out real bad. What if that lady is too much of a wimp for this kind of thing?

The first thing she'll see when she opens the door is this gorefest of a shooting game, playing inside a dark, seedy storage room.

And she'd be playing against a dark, seedy, glarey-eyed *me* for her opponent…No. I should stop thinking about myself. That'll just make me all depressed, and it's not like I have any idea how to improve my life. I'd just start crying, is all.

But even ignoring me for the moment, the content of this game might be a little too much for women or children.

Perhaps I should have drilled this point into Haruka a little more carefully.

The moment I stood back up, no longer able to remain seated and alone with myself, the door opened.

Even though only a few minutes had passed, I still had to shield my eyes against the influx of sunlight. Our first customer was silhouetted in the brightness, making it impossible to see him, which flustered me a bit. In terms of height, I could tell he was an adult male, at least.

It'd be rude not to say anything, so I recited the little spiel I had come up with.

"Uh, welcome! So, um, in this class, we've got a target shooting game! If you can beat me, we've got a wonderful prize for—"

"Heh. You're a girl? I was wondering who I'd see in here. I'd feel a lot better about whipping the guy by the door than a girl."

The man abruptly cut me off as I tried to be as cute and bright in my intro as I could, smile plastered upon my face.

It was so unexpected that I froze at first, unable to process what had happened. Gradually, though, I realized that this man, for all his lack of politeness, sure *seemed* to be interested in some competition.

"Uh...umm..."

Thanks to this disastrous first contact—even in the best of times, I wasn't used to interacting with people much—my heart began to race, my hands shaking a little from the nervousness.

The sales spiel I had prepared had been completely blanked away in my mind. My mouth continued to attempt speech nonetheless, emitting a series of bizarre sounds.

"Can't say I'm too jealous of you right now, lady. My friend told me about his school's festival, so we figured we'd stop on by, and then we heard about this cool game being shown. This guy's, like, *really* good at shooters, so you can kiss your prize lineup good-bye in a few minutes, huh?"

My eyes, gradually getting used to the light, spotted another dopey-looking man behind the first one. Apparently they were a pair.

"Oh, uh, well, I'm gonna do my best at this game, so…"

I tried to retain some semblance of calmness as I smiled in response, feeling the sweat run down my back.

Judging by their introduction, there was no doubt that these visitors were pretty damn seedy themselves. But they were still our first guests.

They probably stopped by the festival just to poke fun at the stalls and have a little laugh with themselves. The so-called shooting-game whiz who showed up first had sunglasses on so I couldn't gauge his expression, but man behind him was practically exuding malicious intent.

"Sure, yeah. I'm sure this is just some stupid homebrew game anyway. Kid stuff, you know? I feel bad for taking all your prizes early on like this, but hey, maybe it'll teach you a lesson about life and stuff, yeah?"

With that, the man sidled up to me and, with a heavy flourish, sat down on the challenger's seat.

"Ooh, you heard him. That guy shows no mercy when it comes to games, you know. I don't know if you've heard of this or not, but he went all the way to the national semifinals in the *Dead Bullet -1989-* championships once. And that's not the only tournament he's entered either, so I doubt a girl like you could stand a—"

At this point in the sentence, the pissed-off guy stopped chatting away and emitted a gasp, or maybe a small, muffled *eep!*-type scream.

That might have been because I dropped the salesgirl smile and put on my meanest-looking glare again. Or maybe he cut his tongue by accident after all that incessant yapping.

"T-Takane…"

I heard a whiny, yet familiar voice. Haruka, looking in from the doorway with tears in his eyes, looked scared out of his wits. These men must have picked on him mercilessly before coming in.

I motioned for him to close the door. Haruka hesitated for a moment, but managed to squeak out a "Good luck…" before slowly sliding it shut.

Checking to make sure it was closed, I walked back to our booth in the darkened room.

Settling into my seat next to the apparently eternally angry guy, I turned back toward the monitor showing the title screen and continued with my explanation.

"So, one final thing I need to mention. This is a shooting game with a point-based system. Whoever shoots down more enemies is the winner. I can set a difficulty level for you; do you have any preferences?"

"What do you think? As hard as you got it."

"All right. Perfect. Now..."

Pressing a button on the title screen, I set the difficulty to "Extra."

Mr. Tateyama mentioned that this level was "so hard, you'd have to be some kind of monster to get a perfect score on it."

"Hey, wait a sec, lady. I ain't accusing you of anything, but you aren't gonna be cheating or nothin', right?"

The eternally pissed dude spoke up again, acting a bit more threatening this time.

I couldn't blame them for considering it. It would have been easy to ease the difficulty for my end only, or to rig the scoring system to my advantage if we wanted to.

"Oh, no cheating at all, sir. Actually, we could change places if you like. It's all based on points, so I won't complain if you beat me from either station."

"This is fine," said the grouch as he removed his sunglasses, "so let's just get going."

"...Certainly. Good luck."

I placed a firm grip on my controller, relaxed it a bit...then gripped it hard again. Making sure I was 100-percent comfortable with it, I clicked on the "Game Start" button.

Enemy monsters swarmed out from the backdrop, completely covering the screen in an instant. The game lasted two minutes in competitive mode. Whoever managed to shoot down more enemies in that time walked away the winner.

The difference between this and single-player mode was that the game didn't end if an enemy hit you—you were shut out of the game for a short period of time instead. You could also shoot certain bonus items to obscure your opponent's view with a giant on-screen blood spatter.

Otherwise, nothing had changed. The gameplay couldn't have been simpler: You see monsters, you shoot them. But that simplicity meant that the difference between a beginner and a seasoned player was obvious to anyone watching.

No. There was nothing "stupid" about this game at all.

And this guy acted like he was too *good* for it. I had to whip him, and soundly.

By the time ninety seconds had passed, I was so far ahead score-wise that my pissed-off opponent had no chance to make up the difference, no matter how much he struggled.

I couldn't take my eyes off the screen so I couldn't see how he was looking, but this was a sorry performance for someone who talked so tough a few minutes ago. I could imagine his expression easily enough right now.

Coldly, robotically, I kept tabs on the monsters appearing on-screen. I didn't shoot any of the bonus items. All I cared about was blowing away my foes.

The end-of-game buzzer sounded, and the game displayed the final results screen.

But the pissed dude, perhaps because he already knew he lost big, was blankly staring at his controller. The guy behind him held his mouth open, dumbfounded.

Of course he was. Slashing apart such a massive number of monsters without a single mistake couldn't be done by gaming the system, so to speak. It was a simple matter of talent.

I had even performed the old party trick of putting the controller down midway and letting myself get whaled upon for a little while. They couldn't say I didn't give them a fighting chance.

"Well, that's the end of the game. Thanks for playing! I'm not allowed to play the same competitor twice in a row, so if you'd like to try again, feel free to come back half an hour from now."

I smiled as I made the announcement. "No way...how could I have..." the angry man said. You couldn't get a more traditional sore-loser script than that.

"Um...if you wouldn't mind?" I said, trying to hurry them out of the room. My opponent immediately stood up and began wildly shouting at me.

"Wh-who the hell *are* you, anyway?! I've never *seen* such an awesome gamer in person like you! How on...?!"

It was such a typical, predictable response. To be honest, I was already getting annoyed by it.

"Well, you know," I replied, "I practiced a lot." It wasn't much of a response, but I hoped it was enough to make them go away.

But looking at my face, illuminated by the results screen shining almost too brightly in the darkness, the men began to rear back a little. Just then, I realized I had made a terrible mistake.

The dopey guy just told me earlier that his surly companion was a champion-level *Dead Bullet -1989-* player.

Playing in the nationals was definitely nothing to sniff at. There was no doubt that I had just trounced a pretty seasoned gamer.

He had certainly demonstrated some flashes of talent during our match, so I doubt his slope-headed friend was lying. But, if anything, I wished that he was.

"Are...are you...Dancing Flash Ene?!"

—This couldn't be going any worse. If he made it to the semifinals—and, especially, if he qualified in the same region that I did—we had probably at least seen each other at the site of the regionals.

What's more, I had misplaced the mask I had prepared for the day of the tournament. I played with my face visible for all the world to see.

I decimated the competition at the semis, easily scoring first place to punch my ticket to the final. They would later call it—and I'm serious here—the "Legend of the Dancing Flash." To say the least, I stuck out a little bit.

I wasn't concerned at first because the semifinals were thankfully not shown on TV, but, man, how could I have known *this* would happen?

I had been generally miffed all morning, so I was putting on this cool, composed gamer-girl image up to now, but this sudden development wiped my mind clean once more.

"Huh? Hey, is this girl famous or something?!"

"Famous? Dude, not just famous. You ever heard of 'Dancing Flash: Eternal Rondo'? That's the guild this lady built. They're, like, legends in the tournament circuit. The scores they put up are nuts. They're in the, like, top three of the team battles—"

"Aaahhhh!! Y-you've got the wrong person! Please, just give me a break! Like, just get out of here already!!"

The man's blabbing away, revealing everything that was in the number-one spot of the "secrets I never want revealed" list, had brought me to the end of my rope.

"B-but...But I recognized your play style! That's, like, the classic 'Holy Nightmare' technique that Ene came up with for *Dead Bullet!*"

I was plagued by the feeling that my guts were going to eject themselves out of my mouth. My face felt like it would start spewing magma at any moment.

I just wanted to stuff these two people into an oil drum, fill it with concrete, and go bury it in some mountain forest.

"That...that's not me, okay?! Uh, please, I need you to get going! Pleeeease!!"

Thanks to this outburst, the door flung itself open, Haruka bursting into the room with a worried look on his face.

"T-Takane! Are you okay—!"

"Yaaagghh!! You go away, too! Please, all of you, leave—!!"

I pointed at the door as I shouted. The three of them murmured "Okay, okay!" as they obediently trundled themselves out of the room.

Sitting back down on my chair, I slouched my shoulders dejectedly. This was a major miscalculation. I never imagined that my true identity would be revealed *here*, right now, of all places...

What would happen if that pissed-looking guy sent me a message later along the lines of "I apologize for being so rude to you earlier. It was a great honor to have the chance to compete against you..."?

He might *do* it, too, is the thing. It'd probably be a smart idea not to login for a few days.

—But Haruka's the real problem. I don't *think* he overheard any of that conversation, but if he did...The mere thought nauseated me.

I always found my handle pretty embarrassing. When the game asked me for an account name, I just kind of freestyled with it. That clan title was meant to be an ironic attempt to sound all spooky and mysterious.

Now it was all revealed...That, and the ridiculous name that people had given to my gameplay style.

"I should just delete my account and die..."

Tears of humiliation came down my face. After all this time of treating him like an idiot, if Haruka found out about how I went around online with all these teenage-fanfic-writer names, he'd probably freak.

My current circle of friends would almost certainly crumble. They'd all politely keep their distance from me, saying stuff like "Oh...uh, good morning, Enomoto..." like someone had just passed gas in the stairwell.

It's all over. This is awful. What the hell is some tournament-level player doing bumping around a stupid school festival like this, anyway? It was just the most horrible luck.

For now, I had to assume Haruka heard everything and come up with the best excuses I possibly could.

But—wait a sec here—even if he *did* make out some of it, it was unlikely he'd understand much of what they said.

No. There was no way he could.

He wasn't a gamer or anything. No way at all.

It'll be okay, it'll be okay.

"Takane, are you okay?"

"Yeah, I'm okay, I'm okay...Aghh! Since when were *you* in here?!"

...Thanks to focusing so fervently on my internal conflicts, I had completely failed to notice that Haruka was there in the classroom, right by my side.

"Since when? Uh…around the point you said you should delete your account and die, but…"

My face instantly ran hot as an oven. He even overheard me *talking* to myself.

And talking to myself about something as stupid and embarrassing as my video-game account…

"No! No, I didn't mean that! You know, the account…like, the thing you use to chat with friends and stuff, right?"

What else could I have meant? Haruka wasn't even listening, but the sight of me, head down, trying to make excuses, would've aroused anyone's suspicions. From the bottom of my heart, I wished someone would throw me in an oil drum and bury me in the mountains.

After a moment, I looked up, wondering how Haruka was reacting. For some reason, his eyes looked alive with energy, as if flames were burning in them.

"You really handled that great, Takane! I thought those guys were pretty scary at first, but they were all polite with me and stuff on the way out! I guess they must've given some respect for your skills once the game was over, huh?"

Haruka was acting amazingly passionate about this all of a sudden.

He was scared and blubbering a moment ago, and now he was going on about sportsmanship like some peewee soccer coach.

But this sudden shift didn't matter. I felt a wave of relief, noting that he didn't mention me once during his speech.

Haruka didn't hear a thing after all. Thinking about it, no way he'd be the kind of guy who'd have his ear against the door anyway. I was all worked up over nothing.

"Wow…They were that nice to you, huh? Yeah, I sure hope I taught them not to mess with this school. Not that they had any chance against me in the first place!"

"Ha-ha! You said it! You know, I was really anxious about all this, but this is actually really fun! You're being a huge help, Takane!"

Of course I was. There were a few unanticipated events, yes, but we had successfully entertained the first visitors to our booth.

And considering how easy it was to fend off a challenger as talented as that was, I was confident we would hold on to our prize—as long as the national #1 didn't show up or anything.

If you focused on the results alone, we were off to a grand start. And if those two guys are already gone, there was nothing left to be concerned about.

Given the location of the science storage room, we could hardly expect to be as crowded as the festival stands outside. I should just sit back, enjoy the atmosphere, and wait for my next challenge.

All this anxiety had made me pretty thirsty. I took a swig from the sports drink I had ready under the desk, a small reward for my epic performance.

"I sure am impressed, though…And that name's really cool, too! 'Dancing Flash Ene,' huh? I'd love to see you show off some of those 'Holy Nightmare' moves sometime!"

The sports drink in my mouth flew across the room, robbed of its chance to tour my stomach.

What liquid that didn't spray out went straight down my windpipe. I began to choke loudly.

"Whoa, whoa, whoa, what just happened, Takane? Are you all right?!"

Haruka gave me a couple precautionary slaps on the back. I would have much preferred it if he suddenly blinked out of existence.

My skirt was drenched in sports drink, and the violent intensity of my coughing was causing my mind to zone out.

If anything, I wanted to just die right there, just as I was.

"Ngh…huff…huff…H-how did…you hear about…!"

Catching my breath, I wiped my mouth with the back of my hand as I asked. But it might have been too late by that point anyway. Haruka had just parroted my handle name and "special moves" (ugh) back to me, precisely, without error.

"Those guys told me. Man, the one dude was really excited about you, Takane! I'm glad I got to find out about it!"

"Ahh…ahhhh…"

I no longer had the energy to wipe myself dry. All I could do was hang my head and groan. It was all over.

Time to wave my school life good-bye. The school festival had been kind of fun, but now it was just another memory I wish I could erase.

"Hey…hey, why're you acting all depressed? I mean, that's really awesome, Takane! You're like some kind of celebrity, right? All those fans! It's like I'm in the same class with this huge big shot!"

Haruka gave me another pat or two on the back, but the term "big shot" mercilessly pierced deep into my heart.

He was right, though. Anyone who saw me would naturally conclude that I wasn't exactly a normal girl. If my hobby was something humdrum like shopping, that would have been fine. Or if I had focused on extracurricular activities instead of all this, people might think I was a really active, energetic teenager or whatever.

But what kind of attraction was there to a teenage girl who spent hours and hours playing a game where you killed hordes of the undead? I couldn't think of any.

Haruka was going on the way he was because he didn't understand my viewpoint. The more he actually found out about my daily lifestyle, he more he'd want to edge away from me, that much was certain.

Then he might not even treat me like a friend any longer. The thought scared me on a primal level.

"Mmm…Well, Takane, I don't know what's making you so worried, but I'm not gonna start hating you just because you're different, you know? So quit acting so down, all right?…Oh, right! Hey, can you maybe teach me a little sometime? I wanna start playing, too!… Uh, Takane? Are you listening?"

Haruka was rubbing my back as he spoke.

Whether he was aware of it or not, the worst thing about this was how he was talking about all this embarrassing stuff as if it weren't embarrassing at all. He probably acted this way with everyone. There was nothing underhanded in his behavior, you could say. That, or you could say he was just too slow in the head to fake friendliness.

Still, through it all, there was something about him saying he wouldn't hate me that I found very reassuring.

Thinking about it made me realize how dumb I was being.

Whether out of happiness or embarrassment, I was starting to feel more tears coming for reasons unknown to me. I was unable to answer Haruka, or even turn toward him.

"Um…Hello? I'd like to have a match?"

Suddenly, another visitor spoke up from behind the door. Oh. Right. The school festival's only gotten started. No time to sit here staring into space.

I hurriedly wiped away my tears and turned toward the door, only to realize that my skirt was still soaking wet.

"Oh…ooh…"

I was frozen, pitched forward like a runner at the starting line. Haruka briskly walked past me and out the door.

There was something generally off about a lot of his personality, but he was always oddly generous to others at times like these.

I took out a handful of tissues from a box on top of the shelf, quickly wiping them on my skirt and the floor.

It wasn't a great amount—just the sports drink I had in my mouth—and it was all wiped up in seconds.

Wadding up the tissues, I tossed them into the garbage can in the room and headed for the door, as if nothing were amiss.

Opening it a crack, I stuck my face out to tell Haruka that I was ready. There I saw our next visitor—a boy, around twelve or thirteen years old.

"Oh, is everything okay? I think this kid wants to play you, so knock yourself out!"

The fire had once again returned to Haruka's eyes. This game wasn't a sport or anything, but in terms of it being a competition where players tried to outdo each other, I suppose there was a sense of sportsmanship to it that appealed to him.

Maybe he understood me better than I thought. The idea brightened my soul as I began to get excited for my next match.

"Oh, are you the champion around here? Well, good luck."

The young challenger, sporting a black parka and dyed brown hair, flashed a refreshing smile that seemed to have something lurking behind it before giving me a polite bow.

"Oh, uh, sure! Good luck to you, too! Here, come on in and I'll explain the rules to you!"

I slid the door open and the boy entered, exclaiming "Coooool!" as he examined the décor.

"Okay, uh, we'll be done in a sec."

I turned back toward Haruka, eyes now blazing with competitive passion, and shut the door.

"Uh, so yeah, here are the rules! We're gonna play each other in the game running over there, in the center of the room. Whoever beats more enemies and scores the most points is the winner! Easy, right?"

I tried to make the best big-sister impression I could as I spoke, the smile that failed me earlier gleaming like the sun. This visitor seemed perfectly normal. Or maybe my first opponent was so abnormal that everyone else seems tame by comparison.

"Whoa, that looks like fun! I guess our little friend isn't here either, but…what do you think, Kido, wanna try it out?"

"Oh, it's a lot of fun, trust me! Wait…Kido?…Wagh!!"

The boy I had just been giving the rules to suddenly began to speak to the empty space by his side.

I had no idea what he was doing at first, but the moment my eyes turned to where the boy's attention was focused, I was greeted with the fright of my life.

Up until this moment, the only person in front of me was this boy.

But now there was a girl, too—about the same height as the boy and wearing a hoodie.

It was too dark to gauge her expression, but the soft "Yeah" she gave in response indicated she was indeed female.

"W-w-where, where did you…?"

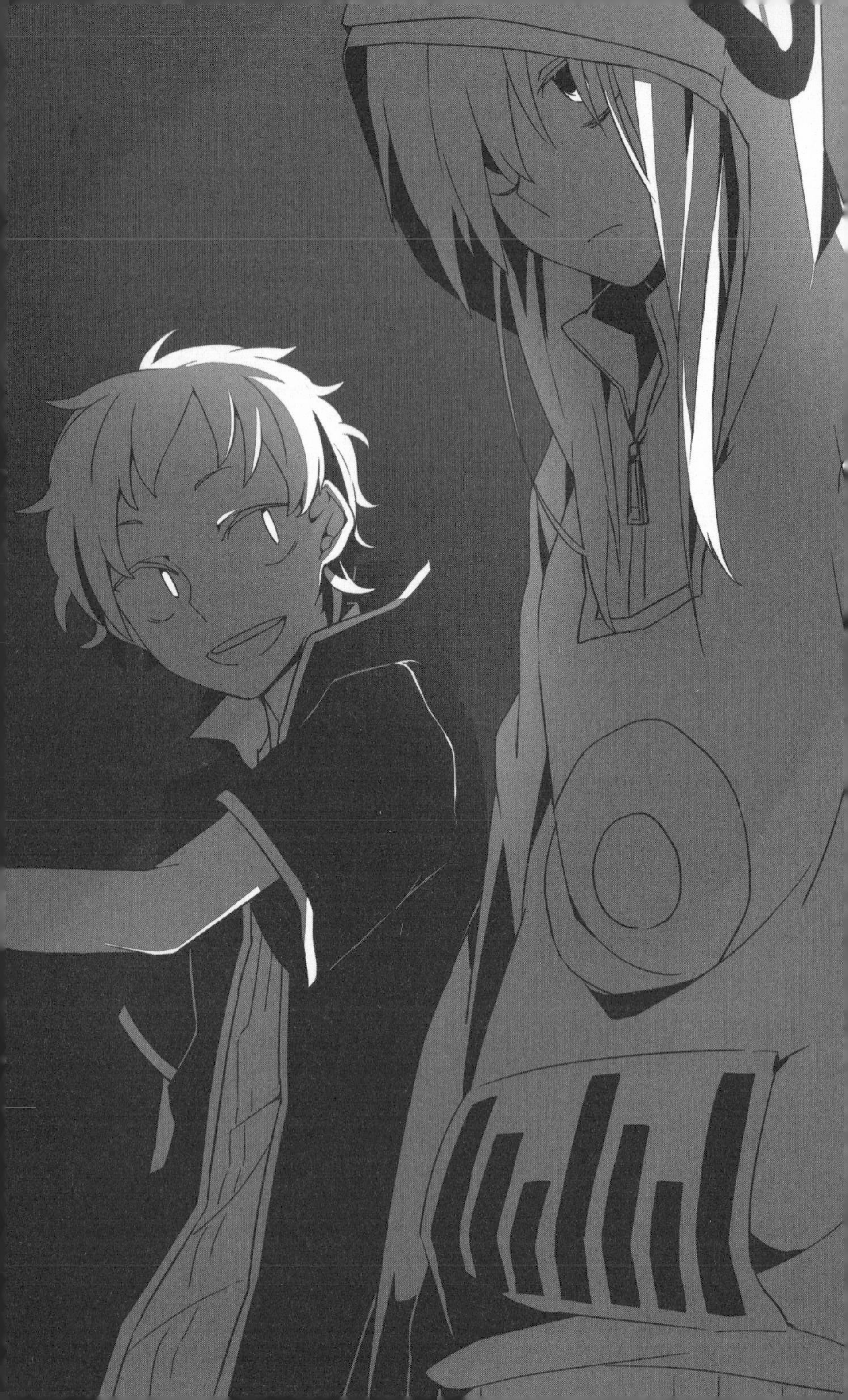

The shock was enough to almost make me lose my balance. There was no way this girl was here before—not here, not in the hallway earlier.

There was no time for her to enter the room, except for the moment I had the door open. Considering that, she had to have gone in with the boy...but from my perspective, it was like she just teleported in, right in front of me.

"You all right, lady? Oh, this girl's been here the whole time. She doesn't project much of a presence, though, so people don't even notice her a lot of the—Oww!"

The girl gave the boy a punch on the side, apparently unappreciative of her companion going on about this...what would you call it? Transparency?

Being a wallflower is one thing. What would it take to be so... unnoticeable? I had never experienced such an odd, disquieting feeling in my life.

—Maybe she was some kind of ghost. The thought seriously crossed my mind for a moment. But that would be even more unrealistic. For someone like me, who steadfastly refused to believe in ghosts or apparitions or the supernatural, the idea that I had just overlooked her seemed far more convincing.

"...Would you mind if we got started?"

"Agh...! Oh, sure, sure! If you could just take this seat here...!"

This girl's existence presented countless questions to me, but regardless of who she was, it seemed wise to get this over with as soon as possible.

Even if she was a ghost, it didn't matter as long as she didn't hurt me or anything. I think.

...She didn't strike me as the evil curse–giving kind of ghoul.

But if she picks up the controller using telekinesis or something instead of using her hands, I'm definitely getting outta here. That was the conclusion I settled upon as I headed for my chair.

The girl and I each took our seats, but my heart kept beating away at a breakneck clip.

Gingerly, I turned toward the girl. The light from the monitor in front of us just barely illuminated her face.

Her skin was pale but attractive, and her hair was on the long side. Her eyes were a bit too sharp and gloomy, but otherwise her face was well-balanced and worthy of the term "beautiful."

But the ambient light was making her look like something right out of a ghost story.

I decided to hurry up and get the game started before I lost my nerve.

"Okay, uhhhh…so, like I said before, this is a shooting game where you try to score as much as you can. If you can beat my score, I'll give you a fantastic prize! So…uh, what difficulty level would you like…?"

"…Normal."

"Oh! Right! Certainly! Sorry! Okaaaay…right! Time to get *starrr*-ted!"

My tongue tripped on that final word out of sheer nervousness. The boy behind us tittered in response.

Seeing him made me feel utterly embarrassed.

A whirlpool of thoughts was churning in my mind, but I just focused on getting through this, and fast.

Setting the difficulty to normal, I pushed the "Start" button. Monsters began to well up on-screen.

This mode offered far fewer monsters to shoot than the "Extra" mode last game, meaning that there were nowhere as many points on offer.

In my personal experience, this mode stuck out to me mainly because the game generated a lot more pig enemies here than in any other difficulty.

A minute passed.

The girl's playing style was utterly normal, with no particular idiosyncrasies. She was just an average girl playing a game.

To me, having just taken on an elite player in the toughest mode the game had to offer, the challenge was lacking. But what should I expect from a regular girl, though?

I occasionally heard her squeak out an "Agh!" or "Whoa!" in response to the menacing monsters, but otherwise she just sat there, quietly playing.

If this pair started going on like "Nngh, this is soooo tough! I'm so terrible at this!" and "Aw, hang in there, girl, you can do it!" that'd be enough to wipe the smile from my face and jump out the window out of pure awkwardness. In that way, things were going far more smoothly than I expected.

But with about thirty seconds left in the game, something strange started happening on my screen.

Suddenly, the pigs in front of me began to disappear, the on-screen gunsight blinking on and off. The game began to bug out in unpredictable fashion.

"Hey...Hey! Is this thing crashing, or...?"

"Don't get scared, Kido!" said the boy between his giggling. "Stay focused!"

I tried to hold out and keep killing foes, but there wasn't much way of doing that if my target reticule was gone.

As time went on, the gap between our scores grew narrower and narrower. Who could have guessed that my going easy on her at first would come back to bite me like this...!

Just as I began to think I was in serious trouble, the closing buzzer went off.

Thanks to my frazzled reaction, I had lost track of my point score. I closed my eyes, praying to myself as the game prepared to show the results.

If she defeated me, I'll have lost our one and only prize to our second visitor.

For the sake of our continued business, we needed to avoid that.

With a musical fanfare, the results screen flashed on. Opening my eyes and forcing myself to read it, I found the WIN mark next to my name. I eked out a victory by a mere one hundred points.

The sweat began to pour out of me. This bug or whatever nearly did me in back there...

But, jeez, Mr. Tateyama! Don't tell me you didn't bother beta-testing this stupid game!

As I thought over this, I heard the boy's now-familiar giggling rev up again.

"Ha-ha-ha! Guess you narrowly lost that one, huh, Kido? Wouldn't be very nice if you won by cheating, though, right? I think you probably owe her an apology."

The boy's face was illuminated by the computer screens as he spoke. It looked like he was trying to hold back tears as he continued to titter to himself.

"...Sorry."

The girl's voice wavered a bit as she spoke. She stood up and calmly walked toward the door.

"Wait, cheating...? I-I think that was just a program bug. She didn't do anything wrong, did she?"

Indeed, there was no way anyone could have called that anything apart from a bug.

It's not like she was hacking into the program or trying to mentally distract me. The girl never even had a chance to break the rules.

The boy continued to beam brightly at me, unfazed by my denial.

"Aw, I'm sorry to confuse you. This is, like, maybe kind of hard to believe, but that girl was actually using her psychic powers there. You can check it out it yourself if you like, but I'm sure the computer's, like, fine and stuff. It'll be back to normal now, so don't worry about that happening again later."

Having said his piece, the boy followed the girl toward the door and disappeared into the hallway without even turning his back to me.

The exaggerated "Aaaaiggh!" I heard from Haruka the moment the pair left no doubt indicated that he hadn't seen the girl before, either.

I put down the controller and listlessly stared at the door they had just left through.

I felt like some kind of fox spirit had just played a trick on me.

That psychic ghost-girl, and that boy who kept smiling at me the whole time...

I've just had this experience which, if I ever told anyone about it, would make then say, "Ah, you've been watching too much anime."

Haruka (as expected) came running through the door immediately afterward. "Was that girl there from the start?!" he asked (as expected). "I didn't notice her at all!"

"Wasn't she there...? I mean, look..."

The display I pointed at showed the score tallies from our pitched battle, the sole evidence I had that she even existed.

*

As the noon hour rolled around, the school began to grow more fragrant.

To the classes running cafés or food stalls, this was the high season. For those of us running attraction-type displays, it was time for a break.

Exiting the dark storage room and hanging a RETURNING 1:00 P.M. sign on the doorknob, Haruka and I set off for lunch.

I played against a dozen or so competitors in the morning, but after that wacky pair, I was blessed with refreshingly normal opponents the whole time, finally making it to lunch without further incident.

"I was really worried for a little while...Like, at first, I thought you were deliberately trying to find the weirdest people possible to play against me."

"Whaa? Oh, come on, Takane! All I did was talk with anyone who passed by the door, so..."

The open space in front of the main entrance, a morass of blue plastic sheets and cardboard a little while ago, was now bustling with stalls and shops run by the school's assorted classes.

From yakitori to hot dogs, from French fries to yakisoba noodles, the colorful signs that lined the area were enough to whet anyone's appetite.

Wandering around as we reflected on the morning's events, Haruka and I spotted an area just to the right of the entry gate where we could sit down and consume our purchases.

"Hey, how 'bout we head there to eat? I eat lunch in the prep room every single day, so this'll be a nice change of—Hey!!"

"Mmh? Whuh?"

I realized that Haruka was already chowing down on some grilled squid, both arms already groaning with food.

"...You could have worked with me a *little,* you know. I thought we were gonna go shopping around together...Like, when did you even *buy* all that stuff?!"

"Mngh...Oof! There we go! Uh, sorry about that. It all looked so good, I couldn't help myself...! You wanna have some, Takane? Here, take whatever you like!"

The bag Haruka was holding contained a vast variety of main dishes—boxes of yakisoba, okonomiyaki pancakes, and so forth.

"Wow...You made some good choices. Okay, how 'bout we go sit down and eat? There oughta be some empty seats at the far end."

I turned around to point out an uncrowded table to Haruka, only to find his mouth already full of the hot dog that was his latest conquest. He nodded emphatically, unable to verbalize a response.

We took seats facing each other in a shady spot of the eating area. The weather outside couldn't have been more perfect for the school festival.

If anything, it was almost a touch too warm outside. Many of the visitors were dressed in little more than T-shirts and jeans.

Haruka and I were lightly dressed as well, since we figured we'd be on our feet for most of the day.

The moment we settled down, Haruka, apparently unable to contain his bearlike appetite any longer, cracked an enormous smile as he laid his purchases out on the table.

The food he showed me earlier was apparently just the appetizer. One after the other, he arranged all the boxes neatly on the table— easily enough food for five or six people.

"Is that, like, a Bag of Holding or something…?"

Haruka looked over his personal smorgasbord, the sheer quantity of which made me wonder how on earth it all fit in his bag. After a few moments of uncertainty, he opted for the okonomiyaki first.

I was pretty hungry myself, so I grabbed a plastic box of yakisoba with sauce and brought it in front of me.

"Well, thanks very much…Oh, right, I haven't paid you yet. How much was this?"

I would've felt bad eating on his dime, so I took my wallet out of my skirt pocket.

"Oh, don't worry about it. You know, Mr. Tateyama this morning, he gave me some money and told me to eat whatever we wanted. Like, ten thousand yen or so. So go thank him, not me!"

"Ten thousand? That much?! Ugh…Our teacher basically embezzled our festival budget, but now he's being crazy generous to us, huh?"

"Yeah, well, I guess he went to a pachinko parlor to take a break from working on the game, and he said he kinda hit the jackpot over there. He ordered takeout from some fancy sushi restaurant for us that night."

Hearing that brought my recently improving opinion of Mr. Tateyama zooming back down into the abyss. The feast before me now seemed like nothing more than the by-products of a degenerative gambling habit, filling me with an odd sense of sympathetic sorrow.

"Hmm? Aren't you gonna eat, Takane? 'Cause if not…"

"I'm eating, I'm eating! Like, how much of this are you actually gonna eat, anyway? You're gonna gain *so* much weight!"

The stalls at school festivals are virtual odes to the art of high-calorie fast food. The sight of the fried-chicken booth was enough to make me start to smack my lips, but if I lost myself in the festival atmosphere today, I knew my body would make me pay tomorrow.

The calories I'd gleefully consume would definitely come back to haunt me in the days to come. That much was obvious.

And meanwhile, here was Haruka, plowing through the plates of boneless fried chicken, hot dogs, crepes, pizza sticks, fries, and chocolate-covered bananas with astonishing speed. The sheer quantities were out of this world, but picturing the churning slurry of grease and bread crumbs in his stomach was enough to give *me* heartburn.

"Well, so? It's delicious. All of it. Oh, and you know, I pretty much never gain weight, no matter how much I eat. I don't pack too big a lunch for school, but this is about what I eat at home, usually."

Listening to Haruka while silently comparing the size of his lunch with his compact frame genuinely irked me.

Even going a *little* overboard with meals for a day had drastic effects on my weight. It just wasn't fair.

"Ugghhh," I groaned. "I wish I could go without a meal or two and not feel so hungry all the time...That, and I wish I didn't have to sleep, either."

"Well, that'd be kind of boring, don't you think? 'Cause me, I really like to eat. And sleep, too."

Haruka stuck another dagger in me as he expectantly eyed a burger he was in the process of unwrapping.

"...Well, I'm glad *you're* happy, anyway."

"Mm? What was that?"

Something about the way he responded, a spot of ketchup on one of his cheeks, made it impossible to hate him. I prayed to no one in particular for Haruka to gain twenty pounds overnight and rip all of his pant seams.

*

One thirty in the afternoon.

After reopening our shooting gallery on time, we were surprised to find our steady stream of visitors from the morning suddenly go dry.

"Weird, huh? I wonder what's going on. It wasn't anywhere near this dead in the morning. You think someone's spreading bad rumors about us or something?"

I peeked out the door and checked the hallway. Haruka was still standing guard outside, waiting for visitors, but there weren't many people roaming the halls at all, much less near our classroom.

As I experienced a sudden pang of anxiety, Haruka reached into his pocket, as if suddenly remembering something, and pulled out a piece of folded paper.

"Oh yeahhh…I think it's probably because of this, Takane."

The paper had a printout of the class presentation schedule for the day.

I lost my copy almost immediately after it was passed out, but I didn't mention it because I didn't want to subject myself to asking Haruka to show me his. Thanks to that, I didn't have much of a grasp of the other classes' plans.

"Oh…? So which of these would keep people from coming here?"

"Well, apparently the student council's holding this thing from one to two over in the gymnasium. I guess most people are over there, checking it out."

The entry Haruka pointed out read "Student Council Project: 1–2 p.m." It was boxed in with heavy lines, giving it higher visibility on the schedule grid.

"Huh. You're right. Man, the student council sure likes to stick out of the crowd, huh? They could've waited until the rest of the class booths were closed up, at least…I bet all the other classes are pretty pissed about this, too."

The exhibitionist streak so clearly presented in the schedule's design was certainly not giving *me* a very good impression of our student government, anyway.

And here I made sure to have a decent lunch and get myself mentally prepped for the afternoon's combat session. Not much point to *that* if no one's gonna show up.

"Ah, it's no big deal. We'll probably have a big rush in half an hour once it's over. How 'bout we just take it easy until then?"

Haruka folded the printout back up, opened the door I stuck my head out of, and entered the room.

"Yeah, I guess so. Man, I wish we could get a real flood of visitors sooner or later. I'm ready to take on the world here."

Just as I was about to stop whining and bring my head back into the room, I spied a figure at the edge of my vision.

It was on the left side of the hallway, near the front student entrance. There wasn't a soul there earlier, but now I saw three men, all sporting the same getup.

They were wearing military-camo pants, headbands, and goggles, as if they had just returned from a rousing game of airsoft and stopped by the festival without changing.

"Whoa...Who're *those* dudes? Are they in costume or something? I guess they're visiting the festival, but is that what they normally wear...?"

It was all a little too perfectly done up to be their everyday outfits. The clothing was one thing, but there even appeared to be walkie-talkies Velcroed to the shoulder straps on the bags they carried.

"What's up, Takane?"

"I dunno...There're these weird guys down the hall. You think we should call for a teacher or something?"

"Weird guys? Here, lemme take a look."

Haruka stuck his head out the door above mine and peered down the hall.

"You see? Really weird, huh? That's definitely not the sort of thing you wear to a school festival..."

"Well, who knows? Maybe that's just the new fashion or whatever. The military look, you know?"

Hearing Haruka use the word "fashion" threw me for a loop. Does he...actually know about that sort of thing? Like, a lot more than I thought?

Maybe these people I was repeatedly describing as "weird" were simply up on the latest trends...Would that mean *I* was the one being weird after all, with my so-last-year teenage look?

"Yeah, uh, I guess you do see that a lot lately. Must be getting pretty popular. Did it start in...uh, Tokyo or something?"

I had no choice but to play along and compliment the drill sergeants down the hall. I didn't want anyone, particularly Haruka, to think I didn't care about looking good.

"Oh, it *is* popular, huh? I have no idea about any of that stuff, so... Guess I should've known you would, Takane!"

Haruka's guileless smile stung me inside. Thinking about it, someone willing to strip half-naked in class would have no business talking about fashion at all.

Yet again, my ego had been kind enough to shovel my grave for me. "Yeah, thanks," I replied, which only served to further guilt my conscience.

"Um...would it be all right if I asked you a question, perhaps?"

"Huh?"

Looking upward at the sudden request, I was greeted by the platoon from before, now standing at attention right in front of us.

They had gotten worryingly close while I was distracted by my inane exchange with Haruka.

"Waugh! Y-yes! What is it?"

Up close, the group was terrifyingly intimidating.

Dressed beyond inappropriately for a high school, they had somehow multiplied since I first spotted them, now a full squadron of six.

Haruka noticed the same time I did. He yelped, reared back, and tried his best to hide behind my back to avoid them. Pathetic bastard.

"I apologize for surprising the two of you. You see, we're searching for this one display...We heard there was a certain booth in this festival holding a shooting-gallery competition."

"Uh, huh...Huh?! Oh, uh, I think you're looking for us, but..."

I was surprised at first by how breathlessly polite this group of young men was, then surprised a second time by the fact they were looking for our booth.

The men began to murmur among themselves, as if taken aback themselves.

"Ohh, this is it, huh? B-by the way, who would our opponent be...?"

The moment they realized they had the right place, the men began to eagerly question me, as if they were about to challenge their commanding officer to close-quarters combat.

"Um? That...that would be me, but...?"

I peeked my head out the doorway just a small distance, trying to keep a safe zone between myself and this bizarre army.

The moment I replied, the group cried out joyously in unison.

The man in front speaking with me even began to sob uncontrollably. What's *this* reaction all about...? I was starting to have a very bad feeling about this...

"P-pardon us, ma'am...! So, so you must be Dancing Flash Ene, then...? It's such an honor to meet you in person—"

That was all I needed to hear. I slammed the door in their faces.

I knew it. They were fans of mine from the world of online gaming.

I should have realized it the moment I spotted their stupid uniforms.

They were dressed that exact way the *last* time I saw them, at one tournament or another.

If I was just a little quicker on the uptake, I could have hidden both my identity and our booth. And none of this would be happening! I am *so* damn stupid!

But how did they know...? Ah, that much was simple, at least. That eternally pissed-looking guy I played with this morning had to have posted something like "Dancing Flash Ene is running a shooting game! Any gamers nearby, check it out and send pix!"

That was the only way I could imagine word getting out. I knew I should have been a lot more firm with him when I still had the chance.

"T-Takane...who were those guys...?"

"Huh? Oh, nobody! They're already gone!"

I smiled through my rapidly beading sweat as Haruka gave me a worried look. Immediately afterward, there was a heavy knock on the door behind me.

"Please! We just want to have a single match with you!" they mewled through the door. "Please! Whatever it takes!"

Who was the idiot who suggested the shooting gallery in the first place? Oh, right, it was me. If I had known *this* would happen, running a maid café would've been a thousand times better.

The commotion on the other side of the door grew louder. Judging by the voices, the squadron had grown into a full company of would-be soldiers gathering here after word got around.

"...Let's get it over with."

With a final oath to myself, I opened the door to find the warriors now numbering a dozen or so. The moment I appeared, a wave of elated cheering erupted across the hall.

I flung the door wide open. "All right!" I shouted. "I'm Ene, and I'll take all of you on one by one! Who wants to die first?!"

"Ene...So cool..." muttered one buck private in stark admiration. The stream of tears indicated to me, once and for all, that the years of my youth were over.

✳

...Two hours or so passed.

The classroom was filled to the brim with onlookers, the crowd spilling out well into the hallway.

Right then, I was in the midst of creating a "New Legend of the Dancing Flash" with the several dozen people I had taken on. The tears, and my sense of humiliation, had all but dried up.

"...She won again! That's forty-five in a row!!"

After what seemed like the eight-hundredth round of cheers and applause, my challenger complimented me and took his leave, weeping in joy at the opportunity to play against me.

The pool of challengers consisted of nothing but gamers now, the general public left to quizzically stare at the events from afar. It was a strange sight, a distinctly non-school-festival-like one.

"You still doing okay, Ene?! We're closing up in ten minutes, so hang in there!"

Haruka, crouched down to my right, had started calling me "Ene" somewhere along the line, cheering me on like a boxer's corner man.

"Yeah...it'll be over...Though it's been over for me for a while now...heh-heh..."

I leaned back in my chair, babbling incoherently. I couldn't guess what kind of rumors would start going around school tomorrow.

Maybe I should just write "Ene" on a nameplate, hang it around my neck, and prance around the school grounds all day.

As I lost myself in dread and idle self-pity, a new challenger sat down next to me.

All the opponents up to now were big, burly (or just plain obese) men, but this time I was taking on a boy in a red jersey, about the same height as the teenage pair who visited this morning.

I was visibly bewildered. Haruka patted my shoulder from the side.

"Ene…I'm sorry to interrupt you while you're in the groove, but we better give out our prize before we have to close. Would you mind much if you let this kid beat you…?"

Haruka seemed honestly reluctant to broach the topic. How long was he going to have the wrong idea like this? I'm not "in the groove." Nothing even close to that.

But, timewise, it might be a good idea to throw a match sooner than later.

Losing to a boy would be something of a blow to my pride, yes, but this wasn't really a competition—it was more of a service to our visitors.

And it sure beats having to lose against anyone in *this* gaggle of gamers…

If I wanted this event to end successfully, now was no time to try to show off. This was the final opponent, besides. I decided to paint a smile on my face for the first time in hours.

"Okay, you're the next opponent, right? Great to meet you! Do you know the rules, or do you need a quick rundown?"

I somehow managed to drum up my "cutesy big sister" voice for him. Who knows if this experience might affect this kid's taste in girls, after all. —I am *such* an evil woman.

"…You know, maybe you think you're good, being number-two in the country and all, but you don't look that tough to me at all. Your moves are so predictable, and you're getting sloppy, too. It's getting me pissed just watching you."

The kid in the jersey didn't even look at me as he spoke. It was the exact opposite of what I imagined.

"Huh…? Uh, I'm sorry, I don't think I heard you quite right…"

I had to have misheard him. How could a cute little kid like this be so harsh with me?

"I *said*, you *suck*. Can we get started already? You can set the difficulty to whatever you want."

—Something inside of my head cracked. There was no mistaking it the second time. He said that I "sucked."

This snot-nosed kid was bashing my play. The gameplay that earned me worship and adulation as the Dancing Flash.

"Uh...you think I suck, huh? So you think you can *beat* me, oh?"

"Sure do. In fact, I'm guaranteed to win. You suck, remember?"

My temper was wearing thin. The blood in my face burned so hot, I was afraid it would burst out of my arteries.

But my opponent was younger than me. There was no point throwing a tantrum over him.

It's nothing that really matters. Just beat him, and everything will be fine. Kids like these are all bark and no bite. Someone needs to teach him that the only thing that *really* matters in this world is the win/loss column.

"Oh, reeeeeally...? I see, I see...! In that case, how about we play a match at the highest difficulty? And just to inform you, I am *not!!...* going to lose."

The controller in my hand was groaning and straining from the strength of my iron grip.

"Wait a sec, Takane," Haruka whispered to me. "You have to lose this, remember?" But I was in no mind to pay attention to him any longer.

—I was staking my pride in this fight.

Right here, right now, the only way to keep my pride intact was to take this kid and his stupid red jersey and tear him limb from limb.

"Fine by me. If you beat me, I'll do whatever you want me to. But what if you lose?"

For the first time, the boy looked me in the face. His eyes were sharp and a bit melancholy somehow. They seemed to see right through whatever they perceived, such was the frigid aura they presented.

"I-I'll do anything you say! Anything! I'll become your servant and call you 'master' and everything! But I'm *not* gonna lose!"

"Yeah? Man, you are so lame. Let's do this."

With that, the boy turned back toward his monitor.

I was agitated, to the point that I knew without checking a mirror that my face was bright red.

I'm gonna beat the crap out of him…! No matter what it takes, he's going *down!*

Taking a deep breath, I selected the "Extra" difficulty and pressed the "Start" button.

"I'll make you regret…treating me like an idiot…"

The duel had begun. The screen began to swarm with monsters.

In the end, I managed to smash my previous top score for the day. My performance was terrific, something I could physically feel, and my sense of focus allowed me to put every ounce of strength I had into the match.

But on the results screen, the word LOSE was printed in blue over my name.

The boy, meanwhile, was marveling at the WIN in gold letters on his screen…as well as the word PERFECT!! in bright red below it.

"You're…kidding me…?"

"Forget about the promise," the boy said as I struggled to grasp the reality of it all. "You'd just get in the way, anyway." And then he left the classroom.

Haruka, flustered, stood up to fetch the fish specimen prize.

"Uh…I gotta go give him this! Ene, that was *awesome,* right up to the end! Great work today!"

I was unable to offer Haruka so much as a single eye blink.

The debating was already under way around me. "Ahh, she let him win!" "But that was her high score for the day, right? Which means that Ene actually lost?!" But it didn't matter to me.

—I was mortified. It was the only emotion I could feel, as I found myself unable to put the controller down.

"Um…listen, I apologize that my friend was so rude to you…"

I was suddenly approached by a girl with midlength black hair.

Today wasn't particularly cold at all, but she had on a red scarf for some reason, making her seem weirdly fragile.

"...You're friends with that kid?"

I placed the controller on the desk. "...More or less," the girl in the scarf replied sheepishly.

Which meant that guy in the jersey, with all that talent, even brought a girl along with him to the school festival?! I could feel pyres of rage about to erupt within me, but the girl's honest, apologetic face quelled the flames.

"Huh...Well, it's all right. He was really good. That was the most fun I've had in a while. But he should *really* watch that attitude a bit more! 'Cause he's gonna have problems if he doesn't."

I snorted haughtily as I spoke. The girl smiled bitterly and sighed.

"I...I guess you're right, yeah. He kind of has a tough time interacting with people, and he's got kind of an ego, too, so...I'll talk to him about it later. Again, sorry about that..."

"No, no, you don't have to apologize...I mean, at that age, we all go through a lot of different stuff, so...just talk it over with him, okay?"

"Certainly. But, oh, he's gone and left me behind in here! I'm sorry, I need to get going. We have to go meet my father in a little while, so..."

The girl bowed her head, then ran out of the room in a hurry.

With our sole prize gone, the crowd slowly began to disperse. Even my fans left the room with undue haste, as if berating me for taking the act too far in the end.

As I watched this take place in my seat, the school clock rang four p.m., the end of the school festival.

The speaker in the hallway squawked to life: "Ladies and gentlemen, the exhibition hours have ended. All classes, follow your planning committee's instructions and begin the tear-down process."

The announcement caused my entire body to be suddenly racked with fatigue. From the moment I arrived until right now, I felt awash in a torrent of unexpected and/or unwelcome events. It was utter chaos on more than one occasion, but now that it was all over...I guess it might have actually been pretty fun.

Now if people can be nice enough to gradually forget about the whole "Ene" thing without word getting spread any farther than it already has...

I pondered over this as I waited for Haruka to return.

I had to hand it to him today. He really outdid himself, helping out around the booth.

Maybe I could treat him to something on the way home...Wait, no. Treating him with my puny allowance would make my savings disappear in five minutes. We could split the tab evenly...No, let's just buy our own stuff instead. That works.

Oh, wait, he probably still has a lot of money left over from Mr. Tateyama anyway.

Better make sure we use it all before he inevitably turns up and asks for a refund.

I put my head down on the table, playing around with the controller in my hand as I waited a quarter hour or so.

...Haruka didn't come back.

He just went out to give the kid his prize. This was taking way too long.

Where on earth could he be, taking all this time?

The click-click-click of the second hand on the classroom clock was the only sound I could hear. After the exhibition ended, all the classes needed to clean their homerooms and head home by five p.m.

We were no exception to this, but it'd take quite a while for just the two of us to get everything squared away.

"...That bastard isn't trying to skip out on the work, is he?"

—No, that seemed extremely unlikely for someone like him. He knew that I'd punch him out once I tracked him down, and besides, he was way too straight-and-narrow to pull something like that.

But if not, then it was unnatural for him to be gone for this long.

I thought over what might be taking up so much time when a worrisome concept crossed my mind.

Could it be that he had one of his attacks while running around, trying to catch up with the kid?

I knew from before that Haruka's illness was life-threatening.

But what with his personality and the way he acted, it sure didn't *seem* that way. I've never given even a second thought about it.

Still, think about it. He's been working day and night on this stuff for the past while, was on his feet all day today with me, and now he's running around like a chicken with its head cut off outside.

The more I thought it over, the larger my sense of dread ballooned. My heartbeat quickly began to accelerate.

I shot up off my chair, accidentally knocking it over in the process. It clattered to the floor with a loud, echoing bang.

But I wasn't concerned about that any longer.

For all I knew, Haruka may be collapsed on the ground somewhere right now.

He might be in pain, struggling, someplace where nobody would notice him in time.

The thought made it impossible for me to just sit there.

I really should have realized it sooner. He was a weak guy. Very weak.

But I never paid him any concern whatsoever. I forced him to go through all of this hard work.

"Haruka…!"

I headed for the door and whisked it open…and as I flew out of the room, my body slammed against the person standing in front of me.

"Aghh!"
"Yeoww!"

I fell back toward the classroom, landing on my rear as I marveled at how far I had sent the other guy flying. I groaned in pain as I looked up, only to find a familiar pale-skinned man lying in the hallway, eyes rolling.

"H-Haruka?!"

"Oww...That was pretty rough. What's up, Takane? You look like you're in a panic or something."

"—You *idiot*...! I was so worried...!"

Filled with relief and concern over knocking him down, I stood up and raced toward Haruka, all but ready to hug him tightly.

—But, noticing the sauce around his lips and the boxes of food that now littered the hallway floor, my emotions converted over to wanting to kick him through the wall.

"...What were you *doing?*"

I rubbed my rear end as I stopped in front of Haruka, looking down at him.

"What? What do you mean, what? The booths are all closed, so I figured I'd grab whatever food's left before they threw it out! I mean, check out all this stuff I got! I could practically cater a house party with all of it! Isn't that awesome?!"

I could feel the anger well uncontrollably within me.

I felt my fists and my cheeks burn. Giving even an ounce of concern for this guy made me feel like such a moron.

"...Takane? Are you mad or something?"

The moment Haruka asked the question, my fist landed directly upon his forehead.

Around the time I hit him, the school speakers reported that our class presentation had been awarded first prize among all the displays in the school festival.

It was sadly drowned out by my angry shouting and Haruka's plaintive screaming, so it took several more days for us to hear the news.

HEADPHONE ACTOR III

There was no longer anyone around me.

The setting sun, cut off from view by the buildings up to now, was perfectly visible from here.

Its light, bathing the entire world in crimson, seemed like a furious flame, ready to burn everything in sight.

Running up a steep avenue, I made it to the apex of the hill, almost out of breath.

On the other end of the headphones, the voice that had guided me this far muttered something to me. But I couldn't make it out. I was too focused on catching my breath once more.

I imagine it was just about the time I was told everything would expire, fade off into oblivion. Or maybe that time had already passed long ago.

But, at top of the hill I had clambered up, there was nothing.

To be more accurate, there was a massive sky spread before me, drawn atop an equally massive wall.

"…No. This isn't it."

I felt a tremendous sense of discomfort. There was something that should be here, exactly what I couldn't quite remember—but it wasn't.

My ragged breath gradually returned to its normal rhythm.
As it did, the cause behind this discomfort faintly began to grow clear.

—It wasn't that something wasn't here.
It's that *she* wasn't here.

"And I thought I could finally *tell* her, too…"

The words unconsciously fell out of my mouth.

My shadow, long and stretched out over the ground, began to dim.
The sun was almost completely below the horizon.

"I guess…I guess this was doomed from the start. This was the last place left, the only place I could have ever told her, and now…"

The words coming from my headphones seemed to speak for my own mind, a mind still unable to recall everything.

"Everything's already over! It's…it's just…everything! All over!"

—It's time to give it up.
I will never have the chance to see her again.
I was already aware of that.

*   *   *

"If...if *this* is the kind of world I'm doomed to live in, then—!"

You don't have to say that, do you?
Maybe you weren't on time,
but at the very end of it all,

—you came to realize where your own emotions lay.

By the time
I turned
myself around,
the city was
experiencing its
final moments.
On the other
side from the
enclosed sky
as it crumbled
to the ground,
I left my final
words to her.
"I'm sorry…
Takane."

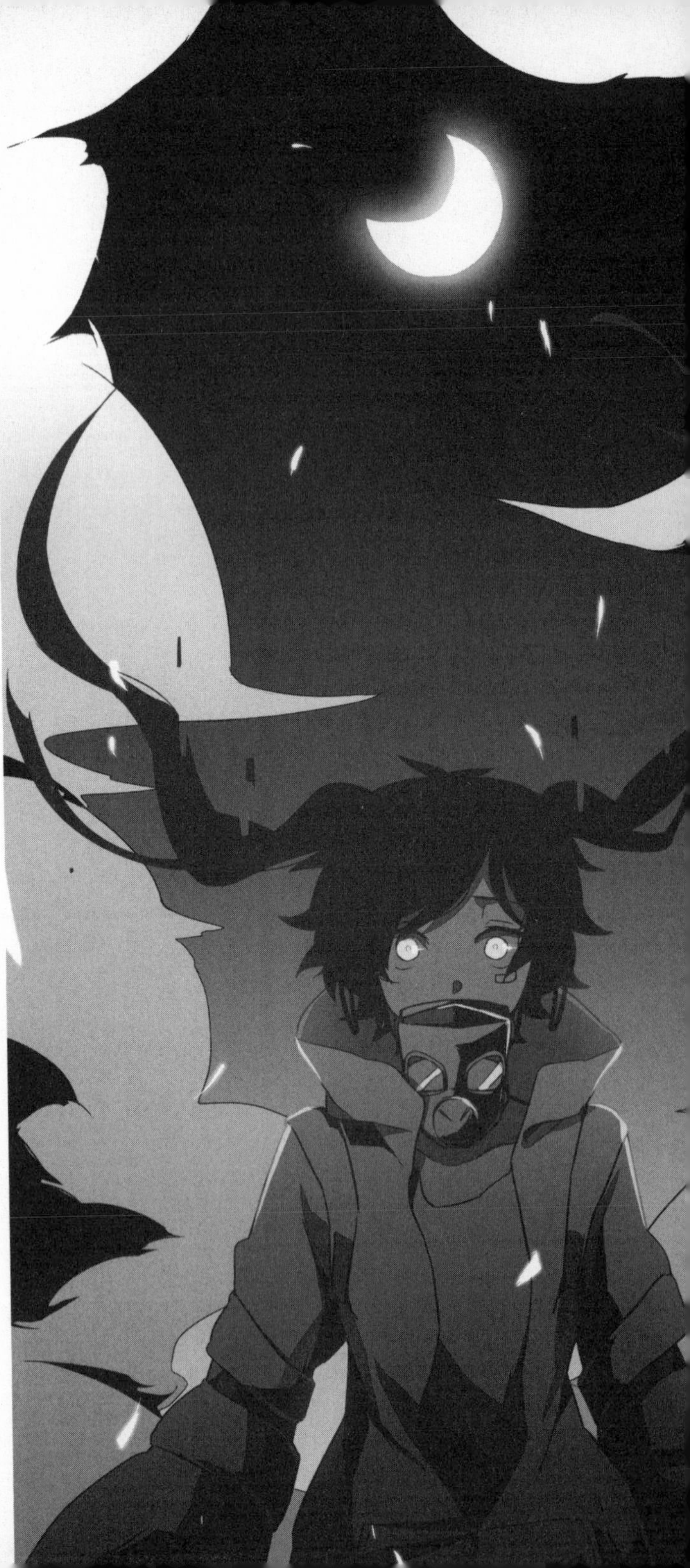

I gazed at
the carcass of
the program
as it burned
itself away, my
consciousness
growing faint.
The words I
heard from the
other side of the
headphones
were more than
enough to lull
me back to
sleep.

YUUKEI YESTERDAY III

The height of summer.

The sky out the window was a clear, crisp shade of blue, a giant cumulonimbus cloud looming from afar.

"...I give up. I don't get any of this at all..."

The austere brutality of summer school was wreaking its full havoc on the classroom.

Haruka smiled briskly as he worked his way through the stack of assignment sheets in front of him, but from my perspective, I was faced with a painful battle, one where I could barely manage to comprehend each individual question.

Weeks had passed since the school festival. We were now both second-year students at the high school.

Which didn't count for much. Our class still comprised merely the two of us, Haruka and me, and regrettably the school didn't boot out Mr. Tateyama and replace him with another teacher for us.

The new school year meant a slow, steady rise in difficulty, and since I (to be totally honest here) wasn't exactly a brainiac, my grades on every test always trended below average.

"Oh, are you stuck on something, Takane? Want me to show it to you again?"

Haruka was already at least twice as many sheets ahead of me, and just a moment ago, I had already tasted the humiliation of having him explain a problem I had no chance of comprehending.

"Sh-shut up! I think I'm gonna have it in a little bit, so just keep quiet!"

I tried my best to focus upon the worksheet, but I frankly had a hard time understanding much of anything written on it.

This was supposed to be a math class, but there was all this English text on it. They were asking me to give not just an answer, but a *formula,* even. It was ridiculous.

"Ha-ha-ha! Sorry, sorry. Not much point to it unless you figure it out by yourself as much as you can, huh? Well, hang in there!"

Haruka raised a fist as he spoke, in a futile attempt at encouragement, before rattling through his sheets once again.

Damn it...He could've spent at least a *little* more time on each of them.

This wasn't looking good. If this kept up, I'll wind up being the only one left in the classroom again.

Once he finished up his work, Haruka would no doubt approach me and ask, "Want some help?" like he always did.

He really *did* just want to give me a helping hand, I assumed, but if I kept letting this happen, I'd lose whatever status I had left in his mind.

So today, just as always, I'll probably shoo Haruka away, saying something like "Just go home! I want to do this myself!"

Ughh...What am I even doing? Thanks to my lack of academic skills and weird stubborn streak, my precious summer break was being eaten away before my eyes.

If my original plan was still under way, I would have spent today holed up inside my room, preparing for the tournament taking place in a few days. Having my time occupied like this was something I never even dreamed of.

"What am I gonna do? I must be *so* out of practice by now...I haven't logged in for two days straight. Maybe I should just skip this championship..."

As I griped to myself, head slapping against the stack of worksheets as I brought it down to the table, Haruka was busily preparing to turn in his own sheets, each one filled to brimming with his handwritten answers.

"Wha?! You got done so quick! N-no way! Are you going home?!"

Without thinking, the words shot out of my mouth, as if the idea of Haruka leaving would fill me with loneliness. In a panic, I tried to correct myself, but Haruka plopped his bag onto his desk, apparently unfazed.

"Oh, guess so, huh...? Well, go stuff your mouth as much as you want then, I guess. I can handle these problems by myself, you know?"

I found myself going overboard trying to act like I didn't care. But as I crossed my arms to drive the point home, Haruka next to me replied, "Huh? I'm not going anywhere," as he took a laptop PC from his backpack.

Shortly he turned it on, typing his password into the login screen like he'd done it thousands of times before. Once he wrapped that up, the title screen of a game flashed on, displaying a white-haired character with a black necklace captioned "Konoha" on the bottom.

"W-whoa whoa whoa! What're you doing?! You're gonna start playing here? Right next to me?!"

"Sure am! The championship's coming up, right? Besides, if I play next to you, that oughta inspire you to get through those worksheets and join me, wouldn't it?"

"No! You're just gonna distract me, and…*ugghhh*, I can't take this anymore! I wanna play, too! Lemme borrow that a sec!"

"Agh! Wait, you can't! I gotta get you to finish that work first! Hey!!"

Indeed—the game Haruka launched was the game I was trying to qualify for in the upcoming tournament.

Ever since the school festival ended, Haruka began to explore topics he had no business exploring, eventually leading him to the realm of online gaming.

I paid him no mind at first, reasoning that he'd get bored and quit within a few days. But Haruka grew more addicted the more time he invested in them. Then he began to post serious results.

Now, he was a fairly famous player in this game, raising his skills to the point where he was actually one of the favorites to win it all in this next tournament.

…And it all started the night after the school festival came to a close.

"…Well, at the end of the day…it was kinda fun, wasn't it? The festival."

"Yeah, well, there were a lot of traumatic experiences for me along the way, but...Ooh! Hey, this steamed bun is crazy good!"

"Ooh, rrrph thinh tha' looph riuhh goohh, too."

"Ew! Stop being gross, Haruka! You could at least *swallow* before you start talking! And Mr. Tateyama, how many drinks have you had? I don't remember inviting *you* in here!"

The three of us—myself, Haruka, and Mr. Tateyama—were here enjoying dinner together.

Haruka had polished off all the food he picked up with astonishing speed, and he and I then hurriedly cleaned all the festival gear out of the classroom, marking a final rushed end to our school-festival experience.

I made sure to kick Haruka every time he called me "Ene" during the cleaning work, but he didn't seem to quite understand that I was angry at him. It served to enrage me even further.

After that, just as we wrapped up the work, Mr. Tateyama appeared as if on cue. "Hey," he said, "the hero of the day always arrives late, right?" I was just as liberal with the kicks for him as I was with Haruka, and to apologize for his late arrival, he made a dinner reservation for us.

"Boy, that's really something, though, yeah? Like, 'Holy Nightmare' and all that? The way you mow down all those bad guys, Ene?"

"I *told* you, don't call me by that name again! Ugghh...I hate this..."

The Chinese restaurant we visited on my suggestion didn't seem to be housing any of the wrap parties held by other classes, likely because it was a fair distance away from our school.

I placed my elbows in what little space in front of me wasn't stacked high with plates, burying my face in my hands as I groaned in agony.

"Hah hah hah! You finally got exposed, huh, Takane? Well, you know, it's not like you're doing anything bad, so don't get so worked up about it, Ene—*oww!*"

I landed a punch on Mr. Tateyama's upper arm and heaved out a sigh before draining the orange juice in front of me out of sheer abandon.

"Yeah! You don't have to hide it or anything! But you know, that name…You took 'Ene' from your own name, right? Like, the first 'E' from 'Enomoto' and the last 'ne' from 'Takane.'"

"Well…yeah, but…but what's that matter?"

"What's it matter? I dunno, it just seemed kinda neat. Like, it seems sort of cool, having another name that isn't your real one. I wanna come up with one, too!"

Haruka's voice was sprinkled with excitement as he eagerly awaited the next round of food. He'd easily eaten enough to feed an entire family and more, and yet he showed no ill effects. In fact, the mysterious forces lurking within his stomach had allowed him to keep his eating pace steady the entire night. It was downright creepy.

"So what about the other one? 'Dancing Flash'? Does that have something to do with you—whoa! Wait, wait! I'm sorry! Just put your fist down!"

I silenced the overly talkative Mr. Tateyama with the threat of coercive force. The clock was already nearing eight p.m., but with tomorrow the last day of a three-day weekend, we still had ample time on our hands.

"Handle names are just something you make up on the fly, okay? You don't have to analyze them like that. It's just embarrassing."

I griped at the apparent abuse they were throwing at me, rapidly pecking away at the chili-infused shrimp put on my plate before Haruka ate it all up.

"Hey, I wanna come up with one, too! I'm Haruka Kokonose, so… how about 'Konoha'?"

"Sure. Whatever. Great to meet you, Konoha."

I gave him as pat a response as I could, but Haruka was unexpectedly and very oddly impassioned by it. "Oooooh!" he chirped. "I really like the sound of that…! I think I'll start spreading my name around tonight!"

*

—Which leads us to today.

"But that's not *fair!* You can't just play by yourself and boost your skills without me…I wanna play, too!"

"Well, that's kinda your fault, isn't it, Takane? I already got all my worksheets done, so…I'll play together with you once you're done, so get cracking, okay?"

Haruka was right, no matter how you sliced it, and all I could do was whine like a child with my "but's" and "come *onnnn's."*

It was another stark reminder of the difference between myself, a below-average student out of sheer laziness, and Haruka, who fully devoted himself to studying but still had to attend summer school with me.

No, Haruka wasn't here in school for remedial classes. Anyone who could finish up those worksheets with that kind of speed would be considered near the top of his class—grade-wise, anyway.

His behavior in class was impeccable, of course, and he certainly wasn't special-needs in terms of the course work he could tackle. But Haruka lagged far behind his peers in one important field: attendance.

In December of last year, Haruka organized an impromptu Christmas party, fielding myself and Mr. Tateyama to help out.

It was right around Haruka's birthday, too, so I remember making a serious effort to pick out a present for him, in hopes of giving him the surprise of his life. I saved up what little allowance I could, forcing myself to go through the heartbreaking task of spending it on someone else. But whenever the image of a grateful Haruka flashed into my mind, I felt an odd sense of excitement about it all.

—But on the day of the party, Haruka had an attack of some sort and collapsed.

Luckily, he was immediately taken to a hospital, preventing any serious consequences from happening.

By the time Mr. Tateyama and I reached him, Haruka was already in the middle of eating his fifth tray of hospital food. Despite this obvious sign of good health, the clinic decided to admit him anyway.

Haruka was discharged after about a week and was back to his usual healthy self at school after winter break, but a month later, he was readmitted to the hospital after another attack.

This time around, he faced a much more arduous recovery, requiring him to remain under hospital treatment for about a month.

But Haruka was concerned far less about his health than he was about the online game he was heavily into at the time. "I have to get outta here and start practicing again," he'd tell me upon every visit.

We both went up to the next class year soon afterward, but Haruka continued to have small episodes of poor health—not enough for a hospital stay, but enough to keep him out of class more and more over time.

Now Haruka was stuck in summer school, making up for enough sick days to ensure he met the minimum attendance requirement.

He never complained about it—"It's actually a lot of fun," he'd say, "as long as you're in class with me"—but I couldn't guess what he really thought about it, inside.

—As for myself…I didn't really know.

"Ooh, hey, there's a new weapon available! Must be some kinda pre-tournament bonus. Oh, man, should I buy it or what?"

There was nothing that indicated Haruka was depressed, at least, as he excitedly stared at the screen in front of him.

Though, looking back, I had never seen him anything even close to depressed. Not even once.

Even when I was the only classmate he had left, even when we were benched from the sports meet he was looking forward to for lack of team members, even when he was forced out of class and into the hospital, he was always smiling.

And watching him smile would always enrage me, exasperate me…and, gradually, enrapture me.

"Hey, Haruka…?"

"Hmm? What's up? Uh, give me one sec, okay? I got a match starting up!"

Haruka was devoted heart and soul to the fight, not taking his eyes off the screen for a moment.

Watching him as he played, muttering to himself in a soft voice, was like watching an innocent child.

…He really doesn't have a care in the world, does he? But if he's gonna stay late like this, it wouldn't hurt him to pay at least a *little* more attention to me.

With a sharp intake of breath, I affixed my gaze back to my worksheet, but the gunfire from the seat next to me made it frankly impossible to concentrate.

This was proving to be no "inspiration" at all. In fact, the distraction was having the exact opposite effect.

I glared at him, entertaining the idea of forcing him out of the classroom, but the sight of him paying no attention at all to his surroundings drained any anger I had within me.

No longer interested in my assignments, I propped my head up with my hand as I rolled my mechanical pencil around. Suddenly, a great idea popped into my mind. I rose up, thrust a hand into the bag propped against my desk, and took out my headphones.

…If I put these on and try to act like I don't care about him, maybe that'll throw him enough to stop playing.

When someone goes into his own little world like that, anyone attempting to do anything with him is doomed to remain alone and unappreciated. And whatever world Haruka was in, it wasn't this one anymore.

Fitting the headphones on my head, I plugged the cord into the phone in my pocket.

I thought a moment about what to listen to, but since nothing in particular came to mind, I turned on the radio app. Light, easy-listening jazz began to play.

Turned away from Haruka, I put my face on the desk, closing my eyes as I turned my ears toward the music.

Haruka *has* to notice this and speak up sooner or later. Then I could fire back with something like "Bother me later! I'm busy listening to the radio!"

It was the perfect plan. I mentally patted myself on the back as a grin escaped my lips.

...But, after a few moments, I heard nothing from Haruka.

For the first few minutes, I serenely refused to think about him, figuring he would talk to me before too much longer.

But once the minutes went into the teens, I came to realize exactly how impatient I truly was.

...He's late. *Really* late.

I no longer paid any attention to the peppy jazz playing on the radio, continually fighting the ever-present urge to fling myself back toward Haruka's direction.

All too soon, after about twenty minutes, I had reached my limit.

"Ugh...ugghhhh...this is so borrrrring. I should just go hoooome..."

I muttered it to myself, not turning around, my last-ditch attempt at resisting the urge.

The sense of embarrassment in my mind ballooned upon realizing just how childish and embarrassing it sounded.

Crap. Why am I putting myself through all of this for *his* sake?

It's not like he's an innocent bystander. In fact, he's being downright cruel, still ignoring me after all this time.

Or am I really *that* unattractive to him...?

This new inroad my mind laid for me led to an odd sense of anxiety. I was gripped by a desire to check the still-silent Haruka's facial expression.

Forgetting my patience at the shock of this sudden impulse, I removed the headphones and turned toward Haruka.

"Hey! Hellooooo?...Haruka?"

Back in this world, with the headphones off and the music gone, the only thing I heard was the in-game soundtrack.

The gunfire had abated, and I couldn't even hear the sound of Haruka jabbing away at the controller.

—Haruka was slumped in his seat, hands spread downward, head flopped to one side...and silent.

*   *   *

"H-Haruka!!"

In a flash, I realized this was an emergency. I stood up in a panic as I shook Haruka's body.

But he didn't respond, his body losing its support as if all of his internals had suddenly gone off somewhere.

My mind went blank. My knees began to shake, and tears began to fall out of pure terror.

"No...no, you're kidding me...! H-hey! Someone! Is anybody around?!"

I shouted out the classroom door as I supported the slumped body of Haruka.

But there was no response. It was summer break inside a nearly unpopulated school, and the area our classroom was in saw even less foot traffic. I wasn't going to be that lucky.

"Please, somebody...Somebody, help...!"

My brain had already grown incapable of making rational decisions. All I could do was hold Haruka's slumped body.

That was because I felt like, if I took my hands off him now, he'd go off somewhere far away, someplace where I'd never see him again.

"Oh, God...!"

The moment after I let out that would-be prayer, the classroom door burst open.

"It's all right," said the familiar man dressed in white,

—as he slowly took a firm grasp on Haruka's body.

*

The hospital waiting room was caught in the grasp of a dark, heavy air.

Occasionally I could hear nurses scuttling to and fro, startling me every time they did.

Haruka had been taken to a large general hospital, built on top of a hill several months ago.

Mr. Tateyama and I sat atop a long bench placed in front of the emergency room.

The handkerchief I gripped in my hand had long grown heavy with moisture, but the tears kept falling from both of my eyes.

"Mr. Tateyama...do...do you think Haruka will wake up? Is...is he gonna get better?"

I threw the question I had thrown at Mr. Tateyama I don't know how many times before.

I knew all I was doing was bothering my teacher with it by this point.

But Mr. Tateyama smiled. "He's made it this far," he said as he smiled and gave me a pat on the back. "I'm sure he'll be fine."

I wonder if my grandmother felt this same way, in the waiting room back when I was admitted to whatever hospital that was long ago.

It felt like you were walking down a tunnel, face turned downward, and the exit was nowhere in sight.

"I'm sure he'll be fine."

I tried to turn my mind in that direction, but the terror I couldn't wipe away forced me to imagine the worst despite myself.

If I had noticed something, anything earlier than I did, maybe Haruka wouldn't be like this right now.

Thanks to my idiotic stubbornness, Haruka was now suffering all by himself.

Maybe, up to the point when he lost consciousness, Haruka was trying to get my help.

And yet I...I just *had* to...!

I had never loathed myself so much before now.

Tears fell onto the hand holding my handkerchief, forming streams across my fingers as they made their way downward.

—No. Someone like me, someone incapable of doing anything, had no right to be near Haruka, no right to worry about him.

What could I possibly say to Haruka when he wakes up?

Could I actually forgive myself for saying "I'm glad you're okay" or "I was worried for you"?

The only thing that mattered to me was myself. Pretending at a time like this that I always cared about him, passing myself off as some pure and innocent thing in front of the plain facts, was just one step beyond forgiving.

If Mr. Tateyama hadn't come for me, I wouldn't have been able to do anything.

I was so powerless, so selfish.

The light on top of the emergency room flipped off.

The automatic door opened, and Haruka's doctor, dressed in surgery scrubs, appeared.

Mr. Tateyama shot upward, running up to the doctor and starting to converse with him about something, but the anxiety and fear within my mind had frozen me to the bench.

Unable to tell what they were saying, I simply watched the two of them as they spoke.

"...I see. Well, all right. Do your best."

Mr. Tateyama bowed his head. The doctor whispered a few parting words before disappearing down the hallway.

"Mr. Tateyama...Haruka...!"

I tugged at the hem of my teacher's white shirt, my mind still a blank. Mr. Tateyama looked a tad relieved.

"...He's still asleep, but I guess they managed to save his life."

He thunked himself heavily down next to me.

The light sweat that covered his forehead dripped down onto his white collar.

Hearing that brought me a great sense of relief.

Haruka was alive. The thought elated me, to the point that nothing else seemed to matter.

But then my stomach was gripped by an intense pain. Haruka's smiling face, the familiar image that had etched itself into my mind, felt like something no longer within reach.

...He might not even want to see me any longer.

Maybe he hated me. He was suffering in that classroom, and I did nothing to help him.

If he was awake right now, I wonder what kind of face he would've made upon catching sight of me.

Dwelling on that scenario made me feel completely, frighteningly helpless.

"Mr. Tateyama...I better go get Haruka's things..."

"Mm? Oh, yeah, I guess we left his wallet and phone back there, huh...? You gonna be okay by yourself, though?"

"I'll be fine...Just make sure you're nearby Haruka in case he wakes up."

I stood up off the bench and headed for the emergency-room reception office.

What am I running from here? Whatever it was, I simply had to get away.

The moment I left the reception area at the end of the hallway, I felt the murky outdoor air surround my body.

The tears just barely started to come back, now that I was alone, but I put on my headphones—still dangling from my neck—and walked on, not taking a single look back.

It was already nightfall by the time I reached school.

The whine of the cicadas had died down compared to the afternoon, the temperature considerably lower from daytime.

But thanks to my hurried pace on the way to school, the shirt of my uniform was wet with sweat, sticking uncomfortably to my back.

*   *   *

Changing to my indoor school slippers, I went out into the hallway, heading down the right side into the lab wing.

The school had grown even quieter than when we left it.

Give it another hour, and it'd no doubt be completely covered in
darkness.

It was funny to think that nearly a year had passed since that crazy
school festival, where we had dozens of people jostling each other up
and down this hallway.

Between all the weird gamer fans clamoring for a match and that
ghostlike girl in the morning, that day was a roller-coaster ride from
start to finish. It was the day Haruka first got into online gaming,
too, not to mention the first time I had a chance to make a female
friend. And then...

"Oh, hey, Takane, haven't seen you in a while. What's up?"

I removed my headphones, startled by the sudden voice.

Turning around, I found a young woman standing there, bundled
up in a red scarf despite the summer weather.

"Oh! Hi, Ayano. Good to see you. But what're you doing in school?"

"Well..." she replied, acting oddly embarrassed.

I didn't know what she meant at first, but for someone like Ayano,
who wasn't involved in any extracurricular activities, there's only
one thing she'd be doing in school at a time like this.

"...Are you in summer school, too, Ayano? Even though you're a
first-year student?"

"Yeahhh, kind of. My grades are already looking pretty dire, so..."

She ejected a strained, creepy little chuckle as she stared down on
the floor.

Judging by her dull, lifeless eyes, Ayano wasn't lying—she must
have been in serious academic trouble.

"...Yeah, I've sure been there before."

"Oh, yeah, I guess my dad mentioned that you were taking summer classes, too, huh, Takane?"

...That teacher just has no idea when to keep his mouth shut. It's not like he has the right to say whatever crosses his mind just because it's his own daughter.

"Yeah, uh, better not dwell on it too much, okay? Not like either of us *wants* to be here, so...Oh, by the way, is he, like, not here today?"

I looked around the hallway, checking to see if the creep who exuded that weird aura all the time was nearby. But everything seemed clear in that respect.

"You mean Shintaro? No way. He's way too smart to be going to something like summer school..."

Ayano's voice notably tensed up the moment the conversation turned toward Shintaro. She was beyond easy to read that way.

"Oh yeah? That smart, huh? That must make it all the tougher for you, I bet...having to deal with that selfish creep all the time."

"Huh? Ohhh, he's not really like *that*, Takane. He's really a good guy, once you start talking to him. Just kind of shy, is all."

Ayano capped off her evaluation with a grin.

Oof. With that kind of personality, this girl's gonna go through a lot of strife in the future. He seemed like nothing but a self-absorbed brat to me, but to her, it must have all seemed cute or something.

"Really? Huh. Well, it'd be nice if he was a little more friendly and outgoing toward others, at least. You know? He must be really happy, having someone like you nearby to spoil him all day."

As I spoke, Ayano's expression clouded a bit for some reason. Perhaps I brought up something I shouldn't have touched upon? That wasn't my intention at all.

"...Nah, I wouldn't be any good for him. He needs someone even more self-absorbed than him, someone with enough energy to pull him toward her. Myself, the best I do is latch on to him from behind. I can't do anything like that."

Ayano squeaked out a laugh and scratched her head as she spoke. I had trouble believing that anyone could be more selfish than that guy. He was headstrong; he thought only about himself; he was frustratingly elusive, never revealing what he really thought about people...Hang on a minute...?

"Oh, no *way...*"

"Huh? What was that?"

"Wha? N-no! No! Nothing! Just something I thought about! But, anyway, sorry to stop you here, Ayano. Better get back home soon, right?"

In a mad flurry, I waved my hand in an attempt to drop the topic.

"Oh, no, I'm glad we got a chance to talk. You know...I was thinking about leaving in a moment, but since we're here anyway, you wanna maybe go home together?"

"Well, I kinda can't...Haruka's had an episode today. Our teacher's at the hospital right now, but I have to go and get all his stuff from the classroom..."

Ayano's eyebrows arched as she heard this. She bowed courteously in response.

"Oh! I-I'm sorry I stopped you, then! You better head back as soon as possible, right? Is Haruka doing all right...?"

"Oh, no problem! He isn't awake yet, but they said his life isn't in danger or anything, and Mr. Tateyama's there for him, so I'm good. Besides...I'd just be in the way over there anyway..."

The words I blurted out pained me inside, proving to be far more self-deprecating than I intended.

Why did I have to say *that*? It's not like Ayano has anything to do with this.

"...Is something wrong, Takane? I mean, no way Haruka would think you're in the way or anything, right?"

"Yeah, but...I dunno. I'd just feel weird, being near him right now. Really, I almost wish I could just deliver his stuff to the hospital and head home after that..."

All this pointless moping was even exasperating me by now. This isn't how I really felt. It couldn't have been.

I shot a glance at Ayano, only to find her normal, good-natured expression replaced with one of anger, her cheeks puffed out just a little.

It was my first encounter with this face, and it startled me.

"Takane, you're being far too dishonest with yourself. With your own emotions. You know full well what you really want to do, but you're pinning the blame on Haruka instead because you're scared, aren't you?"

I was overwhelmed by the sharpness behind Ayano's glare.

"N-no, I…"

"Yes. Yes, it is. You need to see Haruka and tell him how you honestly feel. And also…"

Ayano began to look disconsolate, as if just remembering something.

She took a short breath, giving her time to weave together the rest of the sentence.

"…There are times you want to tell someone something, but you wind up being too late. That's not gonna happen if you do it right now. So try to drum up a little courage, okay?"

Her face returned to its normal serene expression.

"Ayano…"

"And, look, if he brushes you off, I got a shoulder you can cry on, you know? I better get going now."

I thought I had calmed myself down a bit, but Ayano's send-off made my face glow red as my emotions swelled back up to the surface.

I tried to make excuses for myself out of sheer embarrassment, but Ayano was already away, briskly walking over to the shoe lockers.

"Wait, I…I…Man, she really told *me* off…"

I sullenly dropped my head as Ayano left my sight before walking off toward the science storage room.

…How I honestly feel.

I had grown so accustomed to trying to cover it up, I honestly had trouble sizing up what I felt, exactly.

It was too thorny a problem for me. I had no idea what I wanted to do.

Really, it was fine by me if things could be like they were before— the same classroom, the same day-in, day-out routine.

So wouldn't it be best if I didn't try to make any waves? Just kept quiet and moved forward like I normally would?

—I could feel the conflict swirl and churn in my heart.

It's true. This has happened a million times before.

And every time, I'd act like this, not telling him anything about my feelings, right up to this moment.

But is this really the best thing for us…?

The familiar door to the science storage room stood before me.

Every day, I'd throw this door open, and another day full of stress and anxiety would unfold.

I took a breath and opened it up.

"Morning, Takane!"

The moment I blinked…I was struck by the feeling he had spoken to me, but all that was in the empty classroom was the abandoned video game and the mountain of study guides we had left on our desks.

My heart beat loudly and clearly in my mind.

Perhaps this was what I was searching for the whole time.

I flew out into the hallway.

Now I finally understand…

All this time, the thing I wanted to tell him.

And now I can say it.

Yes, I can finally say it now…

A torrent of emotions flooded my chest as I tried to reach him before another second elapsed.

I planted my foot down on the ground—

…or I tried to.

Suddenly, the hallway walls began to warp and bend before me, the floor approaching my head at alarming speed.

My body crashed to the floor with enough force to generate a rebound.

"Agh...ngh...Ah...!"
I had trouble breathing well.
I tried to move, but the best I could manage was to twitch my fingers a little.
...No, not *now*, of all times...!
The fear I had nearly forgotten now held absolute reign over my mind.
At the same time, an unreasonably overpowering sense of drowsiness stole my consciousness away.
...No. Stop it. *Stop* it!
As my consciousness faded further and further, unable to put up any resistance, the last thing my eyes caught sight of was a hazy figure standing before me in the hallway.

—What's that guy doing here?
There's no way he should be here at all.
I was no longer able to discern who it was. My time limit was about to run dry.
Ayano's prophetic words sprung back to mind: "There are times you want to tell someone something, but you wind up being too late."
I am such a complete idiot. I had the simplest of all things to tell him, and I took too much time for it.
Until the final moment when my slipping consciousness flickered out, I kept repeating the words within myself.

"—Haruka, I love you."

HEADPHONE ACTOR IV

Did my last words make it through?

I no longer had any way of knowing, but they must have. It felt like they did.

I felt oddly strange.

As if I was flying through the sky, or was suspended in a body of lukewarm water...

Indeed, as if I had just woken up from something or other.

My near-exhausted breath, my legs racked with pain, the sense of drowsiness that seemed to forever frustrate me...I didn't feel any of it now.

Did I die, I wonder?

Is this seemingly infinite darkness what the afterlife is supposed to be...?

I had imagined something a bit more like a fairy tale, somehow. God must've fallen asleep at the wheel.

He could have at least turned the lights on for me...

"Ugh, this is making no sense at all to...Huh?! Ah! Ah, ahhh...! Wow, I can talk. Nngh...and I...I have a body, too."

I patted down my body from head to toe, but it seemed I still retained full control of my body and voice.

"Okay, so where *am* I, then? It doesn't seem like I'm locked up in a box or anything...Was I just having some kind of weird dream up to now...?"

I suddenly recalled my dramatic, frenzied memories from before.

The city, in a state of chaos.

The sky, crashing to the ground.

The voice, my second "self," that suddenly rang out between my ears...

The mere recollection brought goose bumps to my skin.

Then I realized that I was capable of having goose bumps after all.
Weird.

Why did all that bizarre stuff happen to me, anyway?

I can speak, at least, but it didn't feel like I was breathing at all.

I can touch things with my body, but I don't feel any warmth from them.

If this was proof that I'm dead, maybe I just had to accept it and move on, but there was one thing I just couldn't understand.

What had happened to me before all this, before I woke up in that hallway?

I'd experienced that feeling multiple times before now.

The feeling that I've woken up after suddenly falling asleep.

There were absolutely no memories I could recall from before I found myself in the hallway.

I had probably lost consciousness due to my "illness" before waking up there.

This had happened to me time and time again, so it wasn't anything particularly surprising...but things were a lot different after I woke up this time.

I had never experienced any of these dreamlike events before. And I certainly never found myself wandering in utter darkness.

"Nnngh!! This is making no sense at all! Where the hell *am* I?! Hellooooo?! Is anyone around?!"

I don't know if my shouting had triggered it or not, but suddenly, a square object resembling a TV screen floated up from the darkness.

The screen showed a seemingly infinite number of monitors, as well as a ceiling lined with wires that seemed to snake across each other like living creatures.

"W-whoa! Where'd *this* come from...? What's up with this stuff? Are those TVs?"

*   *   *

Approaching it to take a closer look, I realized it was actually a dark room, something resembling a laboratory.

Every one of the individual monitors displayed a numerical read-out of times and parameters and so on.

Perhaps this square frame I was watching the room through was just another monitor inside this lab.

Not that I had any way of confirming even that.

Total darkness surrounded me. The room I could see through the square, windowlike screen was the only thing left in my world.

I still couldn't help but wonder what was going on in the world from before. I was struck with the impression that the world I lived in had collapsed like some papier-mâché model.

And in the end, I still had no solid idea why I felt so driven to communicate...whatever it was...to whoever it was.

"Hmmm...It's too dark to see much...but I think someone's talking?"

My perception of the room was limited, the light from the displays the only thing illuminating it.

But, while only softly, I could make out some sound from my square window as well.

"...ze One looks like a success, anyway. Hah-hah! I wasn't expecting results like this on the first try. The year I spent preparing for this certainly seems worth it now!"

The voice, audible only by bringing my ear right up to the screen, belonged to someone I knew very well.

"...Mr. Tateyama? What's he doing in there...?"

I changed position to peer as deeply into the window as I could, straining to see who the voice belonged to.

The volume bumped itself up just a bit, enough to make the sound fully clear and discernible.

The dimly lit room, as well, gradually brightened up to the point where I could see everything clearly, as if my eyes had grown used to my surroundings.

But what I saw unfolded before me was a sight I had trouble believing.

Deeper inside the darkened room was a large device, something resembling an X-ray machine.

There was a white, circular gate put in place over a sort of bed, neatly straddling the middle of it.

I saw several buttons, as well as a readout that looked like a heart monitor without any needle. Cords snaking out from the gate had been attached to the body lying on the bed from head to toe, as if plugging in to outlets previously installed on it.

"Wait, is that...*me*...?!"

The person there had to be me. It was in a white outfit, like the clothes you're given in a hospital, and a headphonelike machine was placed on its head.

"W-what's going on here?! I'm supposed to be right here...!"

Then I realized.

This isn't what happens when you become, like, a ghost, is it?

My consciousness is definitely right here, with me. But there's no mistaking my body, either, and *that's* on that bed over there.

Which means...

"Oh, no way, am I really dead...? Oh, man..."

I fell to the floor at the shocking sight.

Then, ridiculously, I mulled over the notion that I could still do something like "fall to the floor" in this...*situation* I found my consciousness in.

How could I have ever known that I would become a ghost—

something you never would've convinced me to believe in, no matter how hard you tried?

Maybe that girl who paid the classroom a visit during the school festival was really a ghost after all, then.

But that guy with her said it was "psychic powers" or something, didn't he?

Either way, I was forced to accept that the supernatural really did exist after all.

But what was more remarkable was how calmly I seemed to take all this.

I was surprised, yes, but my death apparently didn't mean I was rubbed out of existence.

I was right here, thinking to myself and perceiving the world around me, so there was no doubt that I...*existed,* at least.

"...But what should I do now, though? That was definitely Mr. Tateyama's voice. He's got to be somewhere in there. Maybe I could get him to notice me somehow and help me out..."

I brought my attention back to thoroughly examining the room. I thought I heard the voice from my right side before, but...

I pushed my face into the square window as closely as I could, doing my level best to gain a view of the right side of the room.

That rewarded me with a clearer view toward the right, previously a blind spot from my original position.

There was an enormous water tank...or, really, a blown-up version of the formaldehyde tubes you see in science class. Mr. Tateyama was standing in front of it, but I was stunned less by his presence and more by what I saw inside the tank.

"H-Haruka...?!"

I thought I saw Haruka for a moment, but the figure inside the tank was different from the Haruka I knew.

Just like myself on the bed, tubes were attached to his body as he floated aimlessly, head down...but his hair was white, his eyes a light shade of pink.

"Is...is that Konoha? The persona Haruka made for himself? But...but why...?!"

My mind had ground itself to a halt upon experiencing all these unreal revelations, exposed one after the other.
Why was I dead?
Why is Konoha over there?
And what is my teacher even doing...?
I was still having trouble gathering my thoughts when Mr. Tateyama's voice rang out from beyond the window.

"Anyway, the 'key' is now firmly in my grasp. Now I can open up the next 'Kagerou Daze.' But, Konoha...you still haven't..."

Suddenly he was cut off, as the square window erupted into what looked like a vast sandstorm.
I put a hand on the window, wondering what it was. Then I saw that the silhouette of my hand, illuminated by the dim light, was gradually crumbling away at the edges, like a video image dissolving into a blocky mess.

"Ahhh...! Yaagghhh!! W-what's going on?! My body's gonna...!"

The next moment, the word REMOVE flashed across all the countless displays on the other side of the window.

"Re...move...? What, right *here*?"

Not aware of what the message meant exactly, I quickly decided it was ordering me to remove my clothes. I did so as much as I could possibly muster, given that my life apparently depended on it.

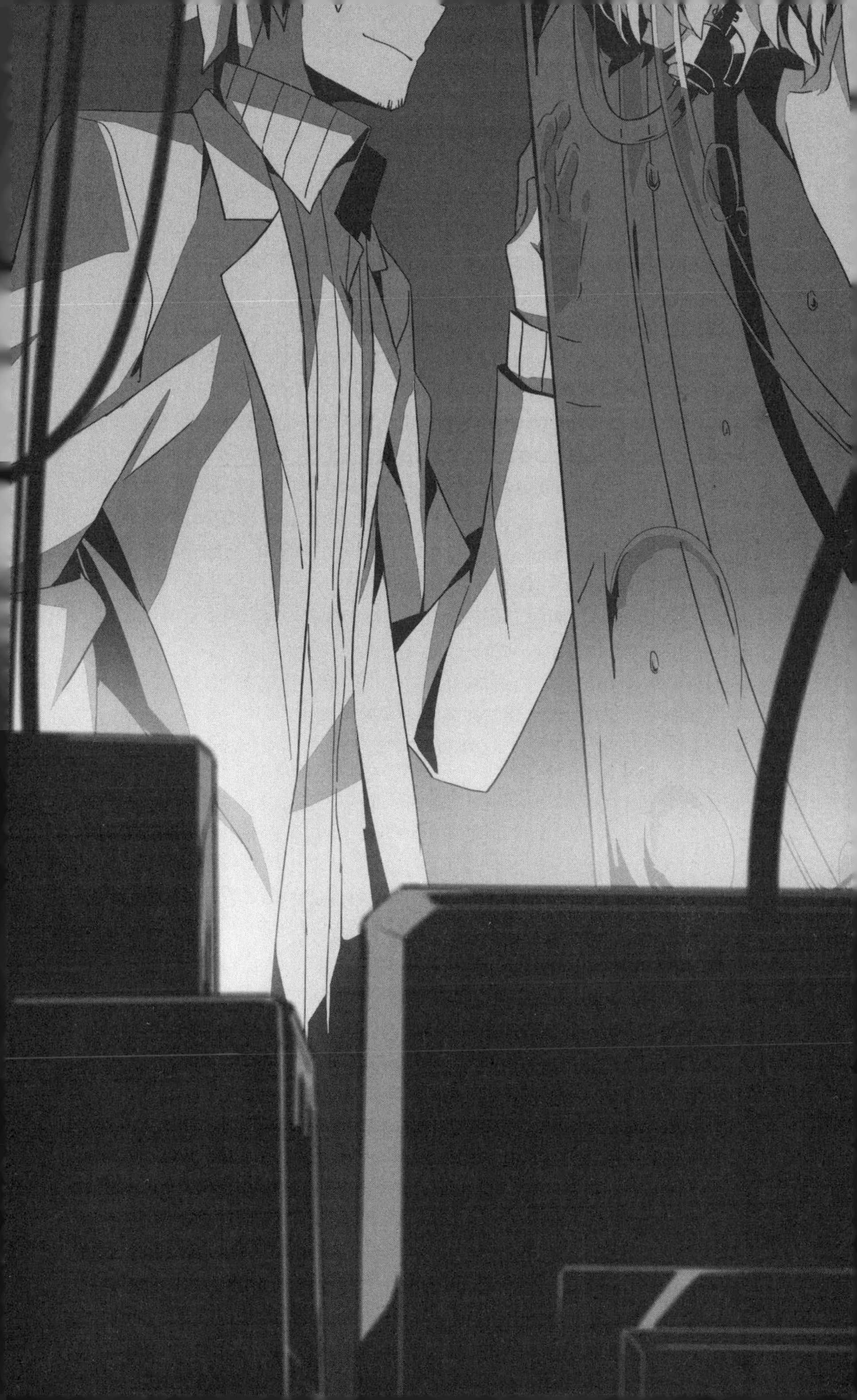

—But nothing changed at all.

So what was that order all about...?!

"Nooooo! This isn't doing anything at all! Ahhh, my feet are gone...!! And my chest...Not that I had much down there in the first place, but..."

As if a bystander in someone else's dream, I looked on as my body dissolved before me.

I was now completely baffled.

But, probably, this meant I was going away. For good this time.

I suppose this means I'm not going to wake up in bed at home, in mortal danger of being late for school again...No, probably not.

As my mind dwelled on silly details like that, my body wiped itself away to the point of almost complete extinction.

I whispered, "Oh, God!" to myself helplessly, but it was all for naught. The next moment—

There was nothing but darkness before my eyes.

"...Ah, my poor girl. You've already lost your body. What further point is there to living now?"

Oh, great, my body really *has* gone away...I mean, I figured it had, but still.

"Even if you went back, there's no place left in the world for you, you know."

Well...well, I'll make one, then. I can carve a niche for myself anywhere I feel like. It'll be fine.

"Well, well, someone's acting a tad too big for her britches, isn't she? That's how badly you want to get out of here, is it?"

Of...of course! I mean, I have no idea at all what's happening to me here, so...

"Well, girl, if you want to get out...then open your *eyes*."

—Wha?!...Like, who *are* you, even?

The moment I attempted to ask, my eyes began to grow searing hot, as if they were burning in their sockets.

At the same time, a bolt of lightning crashed across the darkened world.

I was blinded for a moment. The next thing I knew—there was a login screen in front of me.

To me, this was the most familiar sight of all.

"—Huh! This must have been what he meant, I guess. Okay, then...Better find a place to live, for starters. Someplace where I won't be too bored would be nice."

With my usual speed, I typed my password into the screen.

WELCOME

With the relaxed joy of someone who has just awakened to full consciousness, I dove into the sea of text.

The blue compass began to spin wildly. A sky of zeroes and ones spread out above me, dotted here and there with birds of pure lightning.

—And thus, the tale of my long, long journey through the world of computers began.

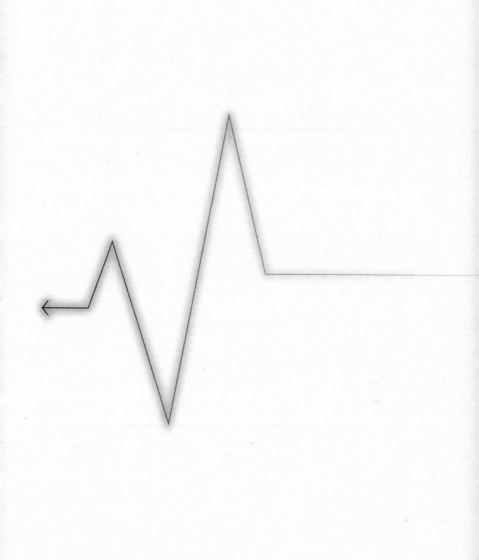

RETROSPECT FOREST

August 15. The height of summer.

The suburban road, well separated from the people and car noise you found in the city, was instead infected with the loud, echoing call of the nearby cicadas.

The long, straight road was interrupted only by rusted-out signs and small houses, dotting the path for what seemed like the rest of the world.

Next to the sidewalk, notably cracked and lacking in terms of solid pavement, the unkempt weeds extended toward the sky as high as they could.

It was well into the afternoon by now. I felt like I had been walking down this path for hours, but I imagine it was only for twenty or thirty minutes in reality.

When you're faced with a never-ending onrush of catastrophic events, time always seems to pass a lot more slowly than it actually does.

—It all started yesterday.

I, Shintaro Kisaragi, have wound up getting shoved out into the outside world for some reason, after approximately two years of the exciting, laugh-a-minute nerd shut-in lifestyle.

Why? Well, thanks to the brazen acts of violence carried out by the evil virus known as Ene, I broke a few of my computer's accessories and wound up having to visit the nearby department store to shop for replacements. That's the simplest reason, at least.

But once I reached that department store, I wound up being on the scene of a terrorist attack—something I had to have, like, a one-in-eighty-thousand chance of encountering. Then they took me hostage, and then they even went and shot me.

…Given the tale this far, I already have some critical doubts as to whether anyone would believe a word of it. But the real story's just getting started. Allow me to continue.

*　　*　　*

After being shot with a handgun, I was rescued by this bizarre organization that happened to also be on the scene.

It's called the Mekakushi-dan, and it's a group of, shall we say, "unique" individuals. An invisible woman, a Medusa, this chameleon kind of guy, you name it.

…This gang is clearly far more of a threat than any run-of-the-mill terror group, but apparently they treated my injuries for me, and by the looks of things, they don't seem like bad people at all.

—So that was all fine and good. Up to that point.

If I had resisted all the urges telling me to poke around this group some more, if I'd just said, "Thank you very much, uh, see you later," returned home, and enjoyed my triumphant return to the nerd shut-in life with gusto, I imagine I could have convinced myself to forget about all the questions I had.

But when the guy they called "Kano" started prattling on and on about stuff, and when I decided to be polite enough to lend him an ear—butting in with "Huh, neat" every now and then, that kind of thing—they decided I knew too many of their secrets and couldn't be allowed back home. The classic criminal gang, in other words.

—I fired back, of course.

Certainly, I appreciated their taking care of me overnight while I was unconscious.

But I wasn't about to blindly follow whatever orders they gave me, and the shock of leaving my room for the first time in ages had fatigued me greatly, physically and emotionally.

Really, even if I wanted to blab about the secrets of this crazy gang to someone else, there's no doubt they'd say, "Yeah, I'd say you're the nuttiest out of all of 'em" in response.

So of *course* I wouldn't tell anyone else. I swore it to them.

…But Ene, the plague-bearing rat residing in my computer, responded just as I thought she would—"Wow, all of this is really amazing, master!" and so on. Thus, she joined the Mekakushi-dan, she and all the secret info she had seized from my PC.

My pleadings were all for nothing. I was very begrudgingly forced

to join the group, and now I'm Shintaro, Mekakushi-dan Member
No. 7.

"Hey, Mom, I just made some new friends! I just joined this thing
called the Mekakushi-dan! They made me Member No. 7! …Huh?
How old am I? Oh, don't tell me you forgot, Mom! I'm eighteen!"

—It'd make me want to die. It really would. There's no way I could
tell her.

"Uh, look, Shintaro, just looking at you is making me feel all
gross…And that outfit is so lame, too."
As I played out my internal monologue to myself, my sister Momo,
who was walking alongside me, spoke up in a peeved voice.

My sister is two years younger than me, making her sixteen this
year. To think that just a bit ago…okay, more like a few years ago,
but there was a time when she acted a lot cutesier to me, constantly
pestering me about this and that for attention.
The moment she became a high-school student, though, her mood
toward me made a full U-turn.
She began to take this domineering, high-handed attitude, the
way a lot of teenage girls do.
Then, thanks to some mistake or other, she actually became an
idol singer, so the point where she's become pretty well-known
among the general public. Posters of her all around town, the works.
I was glad to see my sister make such a breakthrough in her life,
but since the gap between us had grown so large, we barely had the
chance to even strike up a conversation as of late.
But the life of an idol is a pretty stressful one, apparently, and her
agency agreed to give her some time off yesterday after discussing
things with them.
She didn't seem to have too many friends, but apparently she was
chummy with the folks in the Mekakushi-dan, which—though, as
her brother, I had my qualms—was a bit of a relief to see.

*   *   *

"—Uh, hello? Are you listening? Just take that off already. You're drenched in sweat. This isn't some kind of contest to see how long you can hold out."

It was a fact. This temperature, along with the sweat pouring down my body, had made the hoodie I was wearing into a sort of portable sauna for my upper torso.

Taking it off would have been fine, perhaps, but I didn't want my pasty white skin to get sunburned, and discarding this hoodie—this pinnacle, this ultimate culmination of clothing culture—was impossible for someone like me who had grown so fond of that fashion accessory.

The real reason was because this (female) friend I once had said, "You look really good in a hoodie, Shintaro" one time. But now it was starting to feel like a kind of curse upon me.

"Hell-ooooooo? Hey! Are you listening, bro?! I *said*, you're look-ing *gross!*"

Judging by how dogged she was in her complaining, I figured she must have been spewing her frustration at the heat and fatigue or whatnot at me.

I knew how she felt, but, hey, guess what, I'm in the same boat. All this verbal abuse was starting to get on my nerves, so I decided to take the bait and respond to my sister's provocation.

"It's not causing *you* any trouble, Momo. And besides, what's with *your* outfit, huh? Did they make you wear that after losing a bet in some stupid variety show?"

The parka Momo was wearing, with ISOLATED written on it in large characters, was so hideous that even the most avant-garde of celebrities wouldn't dare touch it.

Anyone who caught sight of her would undoubtedly say to him-self, "Wow, that has to be some kind of punishment for something bad she did."

"Uh, what? You don't *get* this? This is *cute*. You have, like, no sense whatsoever, do you, Shintaro? And what about that hoodie? You look like a comedian doing some reality-show bit where he's trying to hitchhike across the country. I can just imagine you getting taken in by some farmer and crying about how delicious his vegetables are and stuff."

Judging by the fangs behind this salvo, Momo was apparently a pretty big fan of her own look, too.

But if I wanted to protect the dignity of my hoodie, I couldn't afford to lose here.

So I decided to strike Momo right where it hurt the most.

"Oh, shut up, Momo. You know, I know what you do every night. You just sit in your room, laughing at Let's Play videos. You know that's freaky, right? Sitting there in that darkened room, eating those dried, shredded squid bits like some guy in his sixties...?"

Momo, stunned by this unexpected attack, began to grow desperate.

"Wha...How?! How do you know that?!"

She may have been all gung-ho at first, but now Momo's face was pale, quickly turning red out of shame.

I continued, aiming to strike a combo blow.

"Oh, you know, I was passing by your room on the way to the john, and I heard this really weird laugh, like 'heh...heh-heh...' You had the door, like, half-open, so it's not like I could avoid seeing you."

Unable to say anything in response, Momo angrily shook a fist at me.

I won. She is, after all, just my sister. No way could she ever beat her older brother.

"You...You're *horrible*, Shintaro! I can't believe that! Plus, I'm sure you're just looking at pervo images that whole time anyway! Ene told me, you know! She said 'my master's sexual drive is limitless'! That's really embarrassing to me, you know!"

The euphoria of victory dissolved in an instant as I was tossed into the bottom of a deep, humiliating pit. I started to break into a cold sweat, easily outpacing the sweat pouring out from the heat.

"Y-you...You...What did she tell you...?"

"Pretty much what I just said!"

"W-what you said...?! Uh...well, look, that was just that one time, okay? That time I accidentally clicked on that weird banner ad! Everyone makes mistakes, you know!"

"Oh, really? How many of them make the *same* mistake multiple times a day? Ene told me that you run out of the room in a nervous panic every time you click on a page, too…"

The emergency alarm within my head began to ring painfully.

I, Shintaro Kisaragi, was undeniably faced with danger. Mortal danger! I wanted to toss the mobile phone in my pocket straight into any nearby sewer grate, but more important than that, I needed to change the topic. Momo was already looking at me like I was a pile of putrid garbage, but I still had to have some kind of chance. Something…something else…

"Hey, what're you two going on about? Aw, it sure is nice to see you two siblings get along with each other!"

"Oww!"

I leaped into the air, surprised at having someone suddenly clap me on the back.

Swiveling around, I saw a large young man in a green jumpsuit, a puffy white mound of something on his back. He flashed us a friendly smile.

It was a man from the Mekakushi-dan I had joined a bit earlier.

Come to think of it, he must have been behind us the whole time. He could have heard that whole conversation…Maybe he was extending a helping hand to free me from this barrage.

"You were…uh, Zetto, right?"

Trying to call him by name when I knew I hadn't quite remembered it correctly was a mistake. By the way Momo instantly landed an arrowlike elbow on my side, I suppose I had it wrong.

I groaned helplessly as the air rushed out of my mouth.

"No, it's Setto! You just got introduced to him this morning! Ugh, Shintaro, you never remember anybody's name…!"

Momo angrily glared at me, as if to visually demonstrate to me how rude I was being. But before she could continue landing blows on me, a peeved voice emanated out from the white, fluffy mass on the jumpsuited man's back.

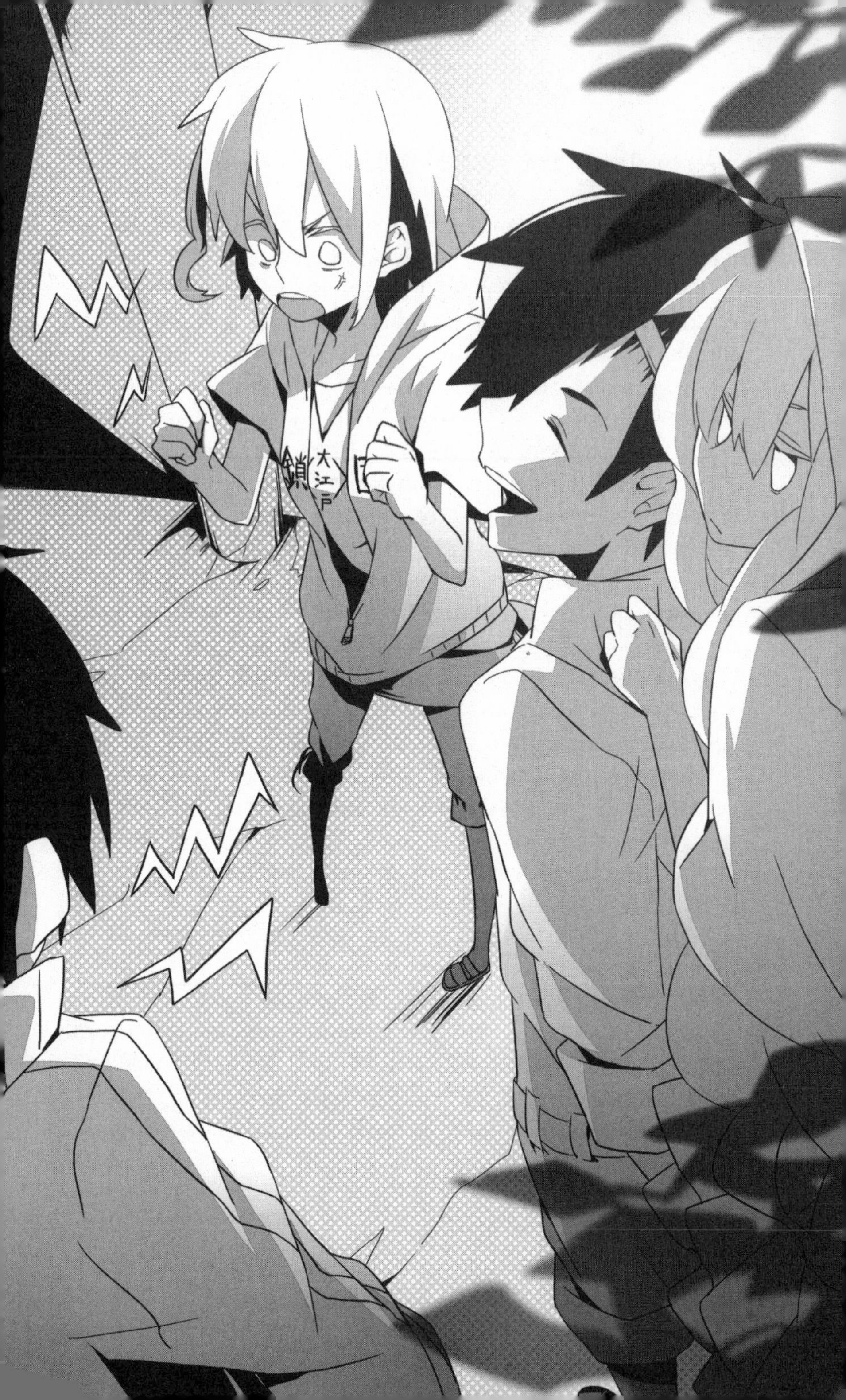
鎖
大江戸

"...No, it's Seto..."

A pair of pink eyes were staring at us from behind the man called Seto's shoulders.

Marie, the white, long-haired mass behind Seto, continued to correct us as she steeled her rankled gaze upon us.

"It's Seto, okay? If you mess up his name...that's just *mean*."

Momo, under the full bore of Marie's gaze, was frozen to the spot like an exposed criminal.

For a moment, I could see her checking on my own facial expression from the side.

"Ha-ha-ha-ha! It's fine, Marie. Besides, I like Setto! Sounds kinda cool!"

Seto tried to appease her, seemingly unfazed by any of this.

Marie remained unconvinced, emitting an annoyed little *mmffff* before burying her face in Seto's shoulder and falling silent.

A moment of silence passed...Momo quietly stepped up her walking pace, trying to ignore everything, but I wasn't about to let her.

"...Hey."

I confronted Momo, my voice brimming with discontent. As it should be. She had messed up the name she elbowed *me* for messing up. That'd make anybody mad.

"What'd you have to do *that* for?"

"Well...well, *you* got it wrong, too, Shintaro! Didn't you?! Besides, I was closer than you..."

It's not a matter of being close or not! Where the hell did you get 'Setto' from?!"

"Ha-ha-ha!" laughed Seto, heartily, as he watched us continue our aimless argument.

We had only met this morning, but already it seemed like Seto never got angry over anything, or that he was too magnanimous to let things bother him in general.

Instead he just brushed it off with one of his belly laughs, leaving Momo and me tremendously embarrassed that we were sniping at each other over this.

"Ngh...I'm sorry that I got your name wrong, Seto...And I'm sorry if I hurt you, too, Marie. Okay...?"

Momo turned toward the two of them and apologized.

Marie's head popped up from behind Seto's shoulder. "Setto," she said. "…I think it's cool, too."

Momo breathed a sigh of relief.

"You know, though, I'm impressed you can actually carry someone in this heat."

"Um? Oh, I'm totally fine. I carry around all kinds of stuff in my job, so it's normal to me. In fact, Marie's easy. She's so light!"

Seto *was* built pretty well. Impressively so, considering that my sticklike arms, the fruits of two years of playing twenty-four-hour security guard inside my own room, were lucky if they could support the weight of a newborn, much less a grown girl.

I pretended that I didn't see Momo out the corner of my eye, looking at me and Seto before exhaling a light chuckle out of her nose.

"But, you know, you can't do that forever, Marie. You need to exercise more on a daily basis, or else you'll keep getting too exhausted to move like this."

"I-I know…I'll try to go on longer walks…"

Marie was down for the count just a few minutes after leaving home, clinging to her spot on Seto's back ever since.

The girl didn't get out much, it seemed.

I felt at least a hint of kinship with her, but in terms of ethnic groups, the difference between a sheltered young girl and a college-age unemployed shut-in was like heaven and earth. My case seemed a lot more hopeless.

The cicadas chirping around us had grown louder and louder.

We were already a decent distance away from the center of the city.

We began to see small wooded areas here and there as we continued down the sidewalk. The number of houses began to plummet.

It was amazing to think how rural things could get after just a little bit of walking. I thought about this yesterday, but it was still weird to me how much the central part of the city had developed.

The somewhat outdated smartphone Momo had in her hand was apparently in its death throes after being doused in tea the previous day. It had allegedly sprung back to life after being tossed into a bag filled with silica-gel desiccant.

"But, hey, I'm sorry for this, guys. Being forced to walk thanks to me…"

Momo drooped her head a little as she murmured the words.

Taking a bus would have certainly been faster, but Kido's "concealing eyes" ability apparently has a weakness—it immediately stops working if someone bumps into any of us. That made it too difficult to try in an enclosed space like a bus, so we walked instead.

Our original plan for the day was to go back to the department store we shopped at yesterday and have fun on the rooftop amusement park, but given the terrorist attack the previous day, there was no way they'd be open for business the following afternoon. Scratch that, then.

But thanks to Ene's selfish ranting ("It has to be *now*, or *never!*"), we decided to head for another amusement park out in the suburbs.

Kido, leader of the gang, and Kano, another member, were going to be a little late, so the rest of us were on our way to the park by ourselves.

Since we were walking down a road with nearly no traffic at all, it wasn't a particular problem for Momo to be visible and outdoors here.

"…Kano told us it was like they made an amusement park out of a national forest…but, hey, is that it? I think it is! I think that's a Ferris wheel!"

Momo, springing to life, pointed toward the right in front of us.

A large forest spread itself out beyond. Among the trees, we could see roller-coaster tracks and other classic theme-park trappings.

"Ooh, it looks like it! Hey, Marie, we made it!"

Seto shook his back to alert Marie. "Wow, we did!" she said when she looked up, eyes aflame with delight. "It looks sooooo great!"

"Ene's gotten kinda quiet, hasn't she? Is she all right? I haven't heard anything from her lately."

"She told me to tell her when we arrived, then shut herself off. Something about wanting to conserve her batteries."

And I had expected another constant barrage of griping and wheedling today, too. It turns out she has a surprising weakness after all.

"Ah. Makes sense. Better get her up soon, then…Oh, is that the boss?"

A sign with FOREST PARK in big letters stood about forty meters ahead, right above a shuttle bus stop. Two of the people stepping off the bus alongside all the families and children looked familiar.

"Ooh, it is! Wow, look at all the people getting off…! I better make a call!"

Momo frantically put up her hood and started dialing.

"Uh, hello, boss? We're right nearby the gate…Okay! Sure, sure. We'll be waiting right here, okay?"

After hanging up, Momo took a quick look around the area. The visitors leaving the bus were herded into the park entrance, not taking a second look at us.

We could see the two people we spotted before walking up to us.

"So as long as we've got Kido's ability, we can enjoy the theme park all we want to…right?"

"Right! Totally!"

Momo beamed from underneath her hood like an elated child.

*

—Out of breath, I found a nearby bench and sat myself down.

It was shaded by the lush foliage above me, making the backrest a little damp and cool to the touch.

I took a deep breath. I guess my sense of balance wasn't working so well…I still felt like I was on a lurching cruise ship, and the feeling of nausea welled right back up my throat.

"Are you all right, Shintaro? You know, guys, you're taking all of this too quickly. You can't just go on the roller coaster first thing like that…"

Seto, seated on my left, slapped me on the back as he offered me a bottle of water.

"Oh, man, Shintaro…Hee-hee! Try not to worry about it too much, okay? Heh-heh…"

Kano, closing in on me from the right, clasped his hands behind his head as he attempted to cheer me up in the most mean-spirited way possible.

"Quit being so rude, Kano. Not everyone's as good at roller coasters as you are. Just because he threw up a bit doesn't mean you should pick on him all day."

"Just...don't say it anymore...Please..."

Seto was just acting out of conscience, but when he reiterated that I had lost my lunch, it served to do nothing but mentally damage me even further. I wanted to die on the spot.

"Sure, sure, sorry. Shintaro's just a lot of fun to pick on, that's all. Gotta say, though, I was surprised to see Marie having such a good time on there. Kido looked all tense, though, like I figured she'd be."

Kano's assessment reminded me of the women in our midst, which made my sense of shame grow even larger. They all saw the whole thing. I'm so screwed.

"Yeah, Kido likes to put on a bold front like that, I guess. This is pretty fun, though, huh? All of us, getting to play around a bit together!"

That was about as profound as Seto could manage, it seemed, as he continued slapping me on the back.

He calls this fun? Me, earning the nickname "Barfman" for life?

"Yeah. It's kinda the first time, too, really. You're busy with your part-time work all day usually, Seto. You were pretty late gettin' in yesterday, too, weren't you?"

"You got me there, yeah...But I tell ya, having all those dudes waiting for me when I got back! What a surprise!"

"I'll bet. Our first new members in years, after Marie joined up. The more the merrier, yeah? And if Kido's happy about it, then so am I. But whadaya think about her, Seto? Momo, I mean?"

Seto and Kano's lighthearted conversation continued above my hunched-over back, forcing me to recall Momo's frigid, aghast face. It made me utterly unable to join in the chatter.

"Oh, she's great! Really polite, too. I was pretty impressed that our shy li'l Marie introduced me to her. And, *wow*, a real pop celebrity, too!"

"Yeah, you should've seen Kido when she brought her in for the first time. That utterly frazzled look on her face...Hee-hee!"

Kano kept chuckling affably, unable to get enough of the mental image. On my end, I felt about ready to cry.

"Oh, and Ene, too! Talk about one crazy character! But what's, like, driving her, you think? Is she being controlled by someone?"

"Yeah, the lady in the phone? Uh, who knows? To me, it looks like she's honest-to-God living in that thing..."

The tears flowed out of my eyes once the topic turned to Ene. She would never, ever forget this incident. No doubt she'd poke fun at me about it until I was six feet under.

"I'd have to agree with you on that one, yeah. You know anything about what makes her tick, Shintaro?...Whoa, hey, what're you crying for?!"

The look on Kano's face as he looked down to peer at me all but screamed "Ooh, look what *I* found!!" He could be downright insidious like that.

I couldn't say I was a fan of the way he breezily put his hand on my back, either.

"J-just shut up! It's nothing!!...What did you say about Ene?"

I mentally switched gears to reply to Kano's question. Maybe getting involved in the conversation would help clear the dark cloud above me a little.

"Huh? Oh! Yeah, yeah, Ene! How'd you come to know that girl, huh?! Did you find her through one of those whadayacallits? You know, those 'casual encounters' sites?!"

"No! Of *course* not! I don't really know why, but since a while back, she's just been living in my computer...I don't know who she is or where she came from. She won't tell me anything, even when I ask her."

That failed to answer any of Kano's queries, but he nodded in approval nonetheless.

"I see...So it's, like, one of those things, huh? You kept pestering Ene about her private past, and then she got angry about it. Right...?"

"No! What're you even asking me?! I don't remember saying anything like *that!* I don't care about her past. If she doesn't wanna talk about it..."

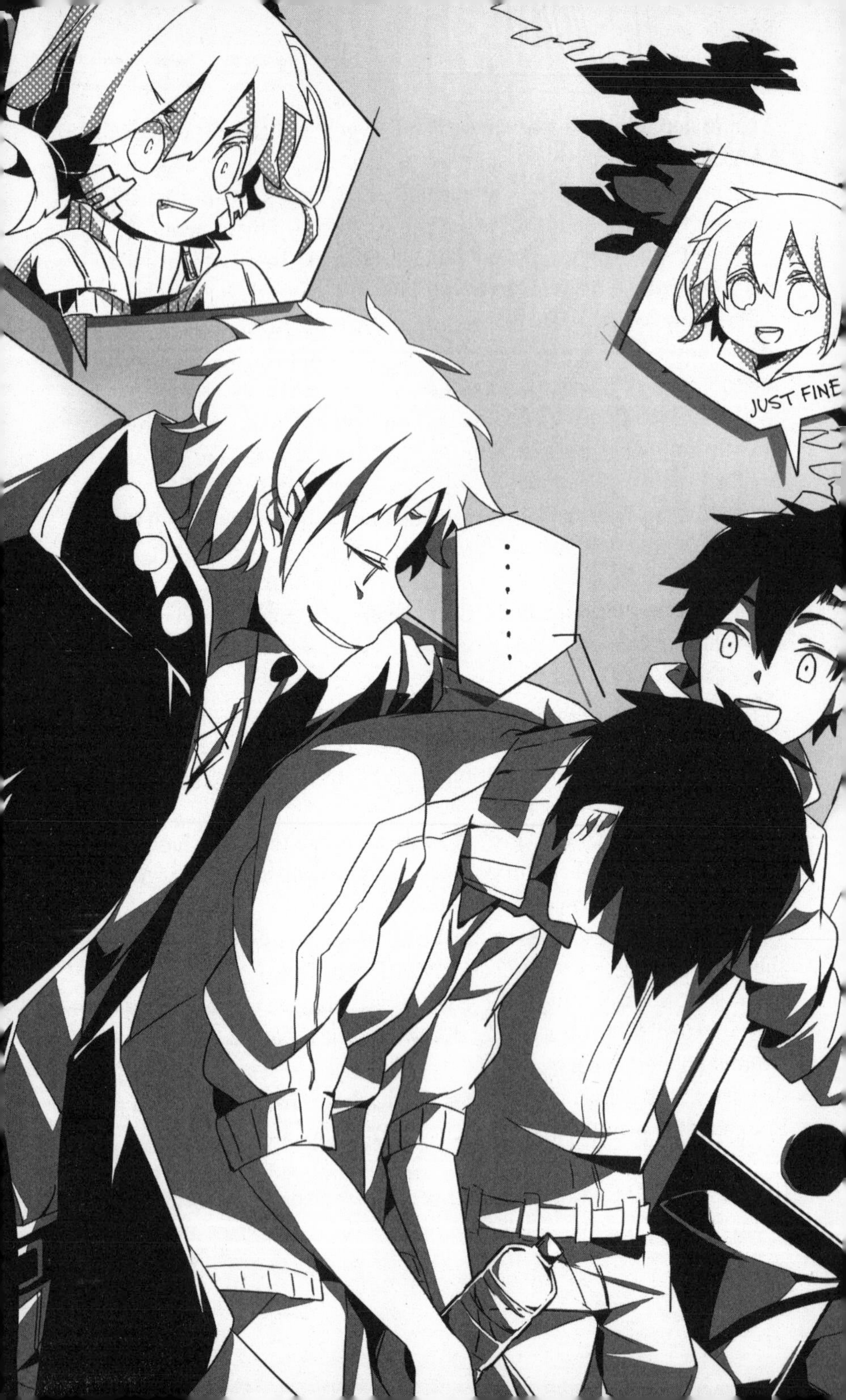
JUST FINE
......

I poked at Kano for his utterly misunderstanding the point. "Hey, just joking, just joking!" he said as he guffawed to himself and slapped my back.

How could I describe this feeling? It's like if you joined this school club, and one of the guys running it is such a pain in the ass around you that you wind up leaving the club in the space of a few days. Exactly like that.

"Hey, hey, let's try not to make this an argument...Oh, you're almost out of water, Shintaro! Let me go buy some more for you!"

I didn't notice until he pointed it out, but the bottle of water I carried was almost empty.

"Oh, that's fine. I'll go buy it myself..."

It'd bother me to get cared for like this all day, so I tried to stand up, only to be pulled back down by Seto.

"No, no, I don't mind! Just try to get a little rest, okay? I wanted to get a drink for myself, besides."

He flashed a warm smile, like he was acting out some lame soft-drink ad, and hurried off.

"Hey, wait! At least let me...give you some money..."

I hurriedly took my wallet out of my pocket, but Seto, already a decent distance away, waved at me and shouted, "I'll get it from you later!" before disappearing into the crowd.

"That's Seto for you, huh? Always running at full blast."

Kano let out a long, unhurried yawn and crossed his arms behind his head again.

I fell silent, not particularly interested in further conversation. If I spoke to him, he'd probably use that as the seed for yet another massive gabfest. That game was getting seriously old to me by now, so I wanted to avoid communicating with him as much as possible if I could.

That, in turn, reminded me of yesterday, when we were both sitting next to each other as hostages.

Even in a life-threatening situation, Kano had been completely relaxed, much as he was now.

Momo mentioned to me that everyone in the Mekakushi-dan was younger than I am.

There *was* something childish, it had to be said, about the entire group taking an off day to visit a theme park.

But given the way they dispatched those terrorists as a team, and given all the unique "abilities" each one apparently had, this was a lot more than just some clique of silly teens.

—But what does this group even *do?* And why did they come together in the first place?

They told me that, until Marie joined up, the group was only three people: Kido, Seto, and Kano.

Now they were at seven, counting myself. And, except for myself, they all had some kind of special ability, or force, or whatever.

Generally speaking, everyone in the group followed the orders of Kido, their boss.

…Aaaand, that was about all I knew.

Ene and Momo didn't indicate to me that they cared much at all about this group's activities, but given that they both had had severe deficiencies when it came to critical thought, I couldn't rely on their judgment.

With that in mind, the way we all joined this group of mystery kids and immediately hit it off without knowing anything previously struck me as oddly dangerous.

It hadn't been that long, but as much as I've interacted with them, they didn't seem like bad people. Seeing them honestly and empathically take Momo's side and worry about her "ability," something I'd never been able to help her with, struck me as the makings of a true friendship.

I didn't want to face the prospect that the group's chief mission was profiteering through some kind of illegal activity.

There was also the fact that, for some unknown reason, the people in this gang knew an eerie amount about these "abilities."

Momo knew that she had started to stick out of the crowd a lot somewhere along the line, but neither she nor I knew exactly when this started to happen, nor what could have caused it.

But the way they talked about it, it was almost as if they knew everything about her ability.

And what does that mean about them? Who *are* they, anyway...?

"Here ya go, Shintaro! One fresh water for you!"

As I was lost in serious thought, trying to unravel the mystery of the Mekakushi-dan, Seto bounced a bottle of water straight off my neck.

"Yeeaagh!! You scared me! Eesh...You could've waited, you know! Didn't you see how I was looking all serious and stuff?!"

"Eh? Oh, well, sorry about that. You just kinda left yourself wide open and all, so..."

Seto flashed me a beaming, totally guileless smile and raised a thumb into the air.

"Wide open? What are you, an MMA fighter?! Ugh, now I've completely forgotten what I was thinking about. Ergh...ah, well. Anyway..."

I now felt a deep, overwhelming sinking feeling in my stomach, as intense as my thinking process a moment ago. I'm probably not well suited for being the "grimdark" member of the gang.

"Aw, c'mon, Shintaro! Gotta enjoy yourself while you're here, right? How 'bout I join you in a little roller-coaster training session?"

I had no idea what indicated to him that there was any chance I'd take him up on the offer, but for some reason, his eyes were blazing like a gasoline fire.

Kano, meanwhile, muttered, "You need to *train* for that by the time you hit eighteen...?" before breaking into a spasm of loud laughter.

"Forget it! I'm not riding that thing again. Not in *this* life, anyway...You don't have to hang out with me or anything, though. Go do whatever you like..."

I concluded to myself that nothing good would happen to me as long as I stuck with these guys.

But he was right. I made it this far. Might as well enjoy a little "me" time while I'm here.

But hang on. Ene was over on Momo's phone right now. If I had any chance to be truly by myself for a change...

"—This is it!"

The moment it crossed my lips, my mind suddenly burned with the overpowering desire to be alone.

As it should. When you think about it, I've been constantly, constantly pestered by Ene this whole time. I haven't had a true moment to myself in ages.

In fact, maybe I should take this chance to spread my wings and focus fully on myself. The opportunity was here.

My mind made up, I leaped off of the bench.

Kano twitched upward in surprise, eyeing me suspiciously.

"Hmm? What's up? What's got into you all of a sudden, Shintaro? Having a heart attack?"

"What? No! Why would I have that? I just thought I'd wander around a bit by myself! Alone! Sorry! See you!"

With that, I briskly walked off and waded my way into the crowd.

Jostling my way through the waves of people, I kept going until I was reasonably sure I was out of sight.

I did it...! I managed to snare some time completely alone, and in the most unexpected of places.

Ah, how long had it been since I enjoyed any truly private time like this?

Thanks to Ene, every moment of my life that I didn't spend bathing or on the toilet was spent in constant fear of something.

If I lay down to sleep, she'd jar me awake. If I went on the net, she'd put up obstacles in my way. If I tried visiting some of the "gentlemen's sites" I was fond of, she tattled on me to my sister...

—But today, I had finally been released from my curse.

*   *   *

I resisted the urge to scream "Woo-hooooooooo!!" with all my might as I took another look around.

With a theme park like this, surrounded by natural beauty on all sides, it'd be easy to find someplace to take a nice nap or something. Wait—if she's not around, I could even play around on the net all I want!

Ahhhh…Heaven on earth. I'm so happy I came here today…!

The world is truly full of wonder. And this is going to be one *damn* wonderful day. I could feel it.

This must be a present handed down from God above to reward all the effort I've gone through to—

"Uh, hey…"

Hey, quiet down. I'm really enjoying myself right now. Don't talk to me.

Ahhhh, what a brilliant day this—!

"Hello? Can you hear me, Shintaro?"

—Being referred to by name immediately brought me back down to earth.

The sheer sense of release I felt had almost made me take a step into a dangerous world, but that voice was kind enough to stop me from proceeding any further.

…Who was it?

I swiveled my head around, only to find a girl with instantly recognizable fluffy white hair standing in front of me, tears in her eyes.

"…Why are you ignoring me…?"

"Huh? Ah, ahhhh, sorry, sorry! Umm…hey, Marie, no crying, okay? Okay?"

Marie was looking extremely out of sorts. Was this just because I didn't respond to her at first? I apologized quickly enough, but Marie's face remained offput, tears still gathering in her eyes.

"W-what're you looking so angry for...? Is there something wrong?"

Marie gave a single nod in response, pointing to the right of me.

There stood a gigantic sign reading THE GREAT ICE LABYRINTH, one of the theme park's main attractions. Next to it loomed a massive building made up to resemble a frozen castle.

"That? What about that? ...Did you want to go in?"

Marie feverishly nodded the moment I finished speaking.

...To be honest, all I wanted to do was tell her "Well, get going, then" and walk off. Why do I have to have my precious free time eaten up by this children's attraction?

At least, the me from a little while ago would've done that.

But! If I said that to this kid right now, she'd probably burst into tears.

...And I knew what would follow after that. It was simple. To any bystander, I'd look like some deranged deviant about to commit a terrible act of violence on this poor, defenseless girl.

I could picture the security guards carting me off already. The ensuing news reports would be plastered with my face, not to mention the keywords "dropout," "unemployed," "shut-in"...

And once things went that far, I was as good as dead in this society. There'd be no talking my way out of it.

"...All right, Marie. Would that make you happy, if we went in together?"

"Yeah! I wanna go in! Can you come with me?"

Marie's face instantly brightened up, her clouded pink eyes now sparkling like flares as they took me in.

It goes without saying that the sight was enough to make the heart of Shintaro, man, shut-in, and above all virgin, skip a beat.

Dammit...I never had a chance.

But, luckily for me, I already boasted a completely full skill set. There were just no free slots left to insert the "lolicon" skill into, sadly.

So much for that upgrade.

We'll talk again once my "virgin" skill times out, though…

—And so, with a guilt-free conscience, I joined Marie in line for the Great Ice Labyrinth.

It wasn't that popular an attraction, it turned out, and judging by the size of the line, it wouldn't take too long to get in.

But something still bothered me. Ever since I…had lost…uh, my lunch, the women in our group had been sticking to themselves, hadn't they?

They hadn't gotten into a…fight, had they? Because if they did, one look at Marie was all it took to believe there were a lot of tears going around.

"Hey, Marie, where's everyone else? How come you're all by yourself?"

"Me? Oh, uh, well, we took another ride on the roller coaster after that, but I got separated because I was standing in another line."

Marie looked away from me as she spoke, staring at the pamphlet she picked up at the entrance instead.

Looking down at the pamphlet, I saw that she was drawing circles with a red pen on the attractions she wanted to visit.

…I-I had no idea she could be so proactive like that. She wanted to hit every ride in the park, even if she had to go solo.

In my mind, I pictured her wailing "I don't wanna go on that unless we all go together" and so forth. Witnessing the truth shattered that image pretty quickly. It was a bit of a shock.

"Oh? Well, Momo's safe with Kido, I guess…but why're you so intent on me joining you on *this* attraction?"

Marie, still deeply focused on the pamphlet, didn't reply. Instead she pointed at a sign near the entrance.

Following her finger with my eyes, I saw a notice posted reading COUPLES ONLY.

Ah. Makes sense. Some of the attractions weren't meant for solo visitors, I guess.

I figured something like this had to be reason for the invite…but, again, learning the truth was still a bit of a shock.

*   *   *

The line slowly kicked into gear, and by the time we were next up, even I was starting to get a little excited. '

I couldn't guess how many years it's been since my last visit to an amusement park.

…It goes without saying, too, that this is my first chance to visit an attraction with a member of the opposite sex.

I took a glance down at Marie. She had already closed the pamphlet, unable to hide her excitement at having the castle walls within arm's reach.

"This…this is gonna be a big labyrinth, right, Shintaro? We'd better drink some tea right now, just in case, right…?!"

"Huh? Well, sure. Just in case, huh?"

Marie took a bottle out from the purse on her shoulder, gave me a nod, and started to drink.

She's got a lot of quirks, but I guess she's really a pure, honest girl at heart…oh, but still…

Dammit…! Get out of my mind, you stupid "lolicon" skill! I said that I didn't need you!!

"Next couple, please!"

The booth attendant opened the door to the attraction.

Chilly air from inside burst out from the door, landing on our faces.

While I was distracted, I guess our turn came up.

I shook away the cobwebs and looked down at Marie. Just as I expected, she was freaking out, too excited to even figure out how to close her water bottle.

"Whoa, Marie. You can put the cap on once we go inside. Don't want to keep the people behind us waiting…"

"All, all right…"

Marie, attention successfully diverted, zoomed through the door.

I followed after, only to find myself rewarded with a surprisingly well-designed and convincing ice maze.

The corridors, lined with icicles large and small, made it feel like some kind of RPG dungeon, something from another world.

The frigid air around us, chillier than what I was picturing, quickly cooled down our sunbaked bodies.

It had to be below zero, by my estimate.

"Whoa! Pretty cold, huh? I know how hot you get all the time, Marie, so it must..."

The unbelievable sight before me stopped me midsentence.

We had only been inside for a few seconds, but Marie was already shivering, the blood drained from her face, her hand still on the bottle.

"It...it-t-t-t's...c-c-c-colllddddd...I'm g-g-gonna d-d-d-dieeeee..."

"...Uh, what did you even come in here for?"

I was dumbfounded. That's...really how cold she gets?

So why did she even choose this attraction in the first place, then?

"I...I, I didn't th-th-think it'd be this c-c-cold..."

"......"

We hadn't even rounded the first corner of the maze, but in her own way, Marie was already about to pass the finish line.

"Oh, come on, it's not cold enough to freeze you to death *that* fast! Here, let me have that bottle, okay? I don't want you dropping it on the ground."

The bottle in Marie's shivering hand was liable to slip away at any moment.

The cap was still open, meaning the contents would all spill out the moment it hit the floor.

And with the AC cranked up as high as it was, any liquid spilled on the floor would freeze on the spot, causing huge headaches for the other visitors.

"O-okay. Th-th-thank...ah...ahh-*choooo!!*"

But with Marie's mighty sneeze, the tea in the bottle rained down anyway—right on my head, bent slightly forward as I stooped over to grab the bottle.

"—Gaaaaahhhhh!!"

I jumped back in fright at the unexpected turn of events.

Getting doused with cold tea in this temperature transformed the maze into a frozen hell in a matter of moments.

"Wh-wh-what did you…Ahhh…ah…sssssso c-c-c-cold…"

My entire body began to shiver in response to the sudden drop in internal temperature.

"Ee-e-eek…! I, I'm sorry, I'm sorry! Uh, something to wipe with, something to wipe with…"

Like an old woman looking for a breath mint in her purse, Marie fished out a virtual arsenal of random junk from her pouch. I could feel the tea absorbed by my hoodie start to freeze.

"Aaaaaaahggghghhh!! My hoodie…My hoooooodiiiieeeee!!"

"Agghh!! I'm sorry, I'm sorry, I'm sorry, I'm sorry, I'm…"

*

It was a disaster. Marie and I had to give up on the maze in the end, but once we were out the door, she disappeared before I could even yell at her.

"Man, she's a *lot* different from how I pictured her at first. A lot more…well, you know…"

I had no doubt she was already getting worked up all over again in anticipation for the next attraction.

Left alone once more, I wandered around the park in search of something to drink.

That little unexpected anomaly had traumatized me, yes, but now I could fully enjoy my free, unhindered private time for—

"Sh-Shintaro…Just who I needed…! G-get over here a sec…"

Someone called my name again just as I passed by a crepe stand. It was a uniquely husky voice, one I could identify well enough without turning around.

"What is it, Kido…? Whoa, where's Momo? If she isn't with you…"

Kido was there, out of breath and sweating profusely.

She had taken the hood off her head—it was much too hot for that right now—and her long hair was free to waver in the wind.

But Momo was nowhere to be seen. Without Kido, her "ability" would make huge crowds form wherever she went…

"Yeah. Kisaragi's kind of gotten herself into some trouble…Please! I need you to lend a hand. Just come with me…!"

Momo, in trouble? I could pretty well imagine what sort of trouble Momo might get herself into, but what could I do to help?

If there was a mob of people surrounding her somewhere in the park, I don't think my presence would contribute much…

But Kido looked like she was at the end of her rope. Her face was hopeful—nothing like what she normally wore, as if I truly was the last person she could count on.

…Well, so be it. Let's head over there and see what's going on.

Besides, if someone says to me, "I need you to lend a hand," I can never really find it in me to refuse.

✳

—It took about three minutes for Kido to lead me through the park.

We stood in front of another attraction, the Haunted Grotesque Dollhouse.

It was the classic amusement park haunted house, replete with gravestones, axes, and all the other standard props lining the mansion's outer walls.

The screams you occasionally heard from inside—presumably from one of the visitors—only added to the creepy atmosphere.

"Uh, so…what?"

I sighed.

"Wh-what? Shintaro, I can't hear you. Speak up!"

It took ten minutes to get through the line.
With three groups left in front of us, Kido put on her earbuds.
Afterward, she alternated between muttering something or other and tightly closing her eyes, as if trying to remind herself of something.

"What, are you scared, or...?"

I relayed the conclusion I had arrived at to Kido, raising my voice enough to ensure she heard me. She arched her eyebrows upward.
"What? Don't be stupid! It's not *that* or anything! It's just that the screaming from the other visitors is annoying me! I-I'm not gonna let some dumb kiddie ride scare me...!"
Kido refused to admit it, but the way she made herself red in the face with her fervent defense made her defense seem less than credible.
"Ugh...So, if I have this right, you and Momo went into the haunted house together, but due to 'circumstances,' as you put it, you left by yourself, and due to *other* 'circumstances,' you can't go back in alone. And since she'll attract crowds if you aren't around, she's stuck in there. Right?"
"Y-yes! Right! Glad I could count on you, Shintaro. You're so quick on the uptake..."
She snorted a little as she spoke, in an attempt to look cool that, in this situation, honestly couldn't have been less convincing.
"So what're these 'circumstances,' then? What reason would you have to not go in a haunted house besides being too scared to—"
"I *swear*, that's not it! That's not it, but...but look, I can't tell you what's in there, okay?!"
That was the most I could extract from Kido after multiple attempts. She had no apparent interest in giving a straight answer.
Considering the way the boss's shoulders shook a little bit when-

ever the attendant at the front door shouted, "Next, please!" I doubted she was useful for much of anything right now.

She was too scared to go in by herself, so she was looking for someone to join her.

I could empathize. Even if she made herself invisible, that wouldn't help much inside a haunted house.

It'd hide whatever screaming she did inside, at least, but going solo didn't seem like a feasible solution right now.

Either way, as long as she refused to admit how scared she was, I didn't have much right to try and convince her otherwise. So I decided to play along.

"Looks like we're up next, boss. Are you ready for this?"

I tried asking Kido in front of the door, but she had already turned up the volume enough that I could hear the music where I was standing. Further conversation was going to be impossible.

The attendant's motions seemed to be enough of an indicator for her that we were next, though.

As we approached the entrance, I noticed that Kido's breathing began to grow more and more ragged.

The attendant opened the door, revealing a room littered with ominous-looking European dolls and blood-spattered antiques—an even more classical approach than what I saw outside.

The moment we laid eyes upon the scene, the sense of fear I had kept a tight lid on up to now began to swell within me.

Kido was already near tears adjacent to me, but I was in no position to chide her.

My own eyes were probably starting to cloud up, too.

The door to the eerie manor creaked itself shut as the house welcomed our apprehensive, trembling selves with open arms.

Once the door was closed, we were shut off from all outside light, the scene ominously lit by flickering candles and lamps.

A chill air, cold in a different way from the ice maze earlier, cooled our bodies up from our legs.

We were both overwhelmed by the scene, finding ourselves already all but unable to press forward.

"Huh...huh. They did a pretty good job...huh, Kido...?"

I turned around, holding my arm steady against the trembling fingers of the girl next to me, only to find Kido's eyes shut tightly as she attempted to lose herself in the world of her music. I plucked the earbuds out of her head and confiscated them, along with the music player in her pocket.

"Aaghhh!! What're you doing, Shintaro?! G-g-give it back, now!"

"What are you, stupid? How are we supposed to find Momo if I can't even talk to you?!"

"I-I know that...but..."

The earbudless Kido began to visibly shiver, like a newborn goat. The sight of the normally composed, above-it-all boss now reduced to sheer uselessness made things all the more anxious for me.

But standing still wasn't going to accomplish anything.

If we wanted to get out of here quickly, we had to keep pushing our legs forward, nose to the grindstone.

I somehow got myself off and walking, Kido following a step behind.

Thanks to the uniquely haunted house–like smells and soundtrack, the path we made slow yet steady progress through was, in a word, terrifying.

The hanging scythes and portraits of headless dolls lining the hallway fanned the fear within us that those blades could come flying forward at any moment.

I squinted, attempting to keep them out of sight as much as I could, and tried to crouch down as I continued.

Kido copied my stance as she followed behind. It probably looked ridiculous, someone our age acting like this, but I didn't care. We were fighting for our lives here.

*　　*　　*

"…Hey, didn't you already go through this once? You already know, like, what's gonna come out and everything, right?"

I turned around to look at Kido after realizing it, but she had her eyes shut and her hands against her ears, all but broadcasting that she didn't want to talk right now.

"Geez, you don't have to ignore me," I said as I extended a hand to Kido. The moment I did, one of the dolls tossed aside in the corridor began to speak.

"Yeeaaagghhh!! What the hell?!"

"The master of this mansion was a world-famous doll collector. But one day, he *changed*. He began inviting guests into his house… and murdering them so he could turn them into dolls! But I wonder if *you'll* be able to make it out alive? Hee-hee-hee-hee-hee!!"

I reeled backward, my heart about to leap out of my chest, and slumped down to the floor.

You call *that* guy a murderer? I'm so delicate, I'm gonna die of shock thanks to *your* little performance long before I run into him.

Kido, standing next to my slumped-over self, had an expression of relief on her face as she removed her hands from her ears and stared down at me piteously.

"You…you had to have known about that…Is that why you covered your ears…?!"

"Oh, um, sorry. I wanted to tell you, but I was too busy keeping my ears…uh, I mean, it'd be more fun if it was fresh for you, too, after all, so…"

The sudden left turn Kido made midresponse did not go unnoticed.

"Fun, my ass! You were freaking out and covering your ears!"

"I-I'm not freaking out, okay?! I just happened to be…!"

As she spoke, Kido noticed something in the distance, then quickly made her way deeper down the corridor.

Has she experienced some sort of instantaneous freedom from

her anxieties? No, probably not. Judging by her behavior so far, she couldn't be *more* freaking out right now.

So, what…?

As I thought it over, a terrible premonition began to haunt me.

Slowing turning back the way we walked in from, I saw a group of people lumbering toward me, their clothes covered in blood, no doubt the hapless guests brutally murdered by the master of the house.

"Aaaaaaaaahhhhh!! I'm sorry, I'm sorry! Please, let me go!!"

With lightning-fast reflexes, I prostrated myself before the horde of zombies, then—reconsidering this tactic—sprang upward and sped away in the opposite direction. Where did *those* bastards come from?! I guess they were extras working for the haunted house, but their performance was so convincing, they left me literally begging for my life.

I quickly caught up to Kido ahead of me, just in time to see her arm being grabbed by countless hands coming out from the wall. Her eyes had lolled almost all the way back inside her head.

"Aaghh! L-let go! Stop it!"

Kido was shouting at the top of her lungs, wholly forgetting that this was supposed to be entertainment.

Once she did, the extras on the other side of the wall pulled their hands back.

Good job, guys. Don't come back again, please.

"Huff…huff…Sorry about that, Shintaro. Thanks for the help…"

"Yeah, how about you stop running away from me like that, all right?! That was really scary!"

"Huh? Oh. Yeah, sorry. I just remembered this errand I had to run…"

Kido awkwardly averted her eyes as she spoke.

—Man, there's something *up* with this girl. Talk about someone I can't count on in a pinch.

*   *   *

"So where did you get separated from Momo? Up ahead some more?"
"…Uh, r-right around the next corner. I think…"

Passing through the hands-in-the-wall zone, I turned the corner Kido pointed out, only to find the corridor ahead lined with large piles of coffins…The owner of this place turned his visitors into dolls, didn't he?

So what's he even need coffins for, anyway?

Of course, if I was going to start pointing out issues with this house, the zombies didn't make much sense either. The hands popping out of the walls? Even more off-spec.

There was a lot about this house you could make fun of, really. And look at the two of us, about ready to pee our pants in the middle of it. Putting it out of my mind, I moved onward. Behind one of the mountains of coffins on the right, I spotted a flash of brown hair.

"…There she is!"

Kido took several steps backward in fear.
"Th-th-there *what* is?! W-where is she? Hey! Shintaro!"
"It's not a ghost or anything! I mean that Momo's hiding in here!"

I pointed it out, giving Kido a chance to see Momo's hair for herself. She breathed a sigh of relief.
"Oh, it's Kisaragi…Well, good thing we finally tracked her down. Thanks for your help, Shintaro."

Kido stuck her hands in the pockets of her parka in a failed attempt to play it cool. It seemed like a gag by this point.

"B-boss…"
We heard Momo's voice croak out from inside the coffin. I imagined she was waiting for Kido to come back for her before she dared emerge from it.

…I wondered what she was waiting for. She wasn't *that* far away, and besides, it was only the three of us in here.

"Hey, Kisaragi!" Kido said as she approached the coffins. "It's me! Sorry I left you behind. Let's hurry up and get…!!"

One look at Momo after she turned around was enough to make Kido faint on the spot.

I was pretty surprised, too, looking on from afar, but I figure I deserve a medal for not screaming out loud, at least.

"Uh…huh? Boss?! Did, did I frighten you too much…?"

Momo's face was splattered with blood as she climbed out of the coffin, an axe embedded in her skull.

What's worse, she was actually trying to give Kido a hug in that makeup. In Kido's eyes, she must have been a possessed monster ready to pounce on her.

"Momo, are you crazy…?"

She turned toward me as I approached.

The look was even scarier up close.

"Whoa! You actually went in here, bro? You're such a fraidy-cat usually…"

Momo honestly looked surprised underneath all the fake blood covering her face.

"I can handle a stupid amusement park haunted house, Momo! But what's with that? Why're you all done up like that?"

"Oh, this? Well, you know, the boss left me behind, so I hid behind those coffins, but then I found this axe prop, so I figured I'd take advantage and give the boss a scare once she came back. So I put on this makeup, and I've been waiting here since. I didn't think it'd be *that* effective…"

I have to hand it to my sister. She's so scary, she can make the boss faint at a single glance.

But an unconscious Kido meant that we were now no closer to getting out of here.

"Well, *now* what're you gonna do?! We're still suck in here!"

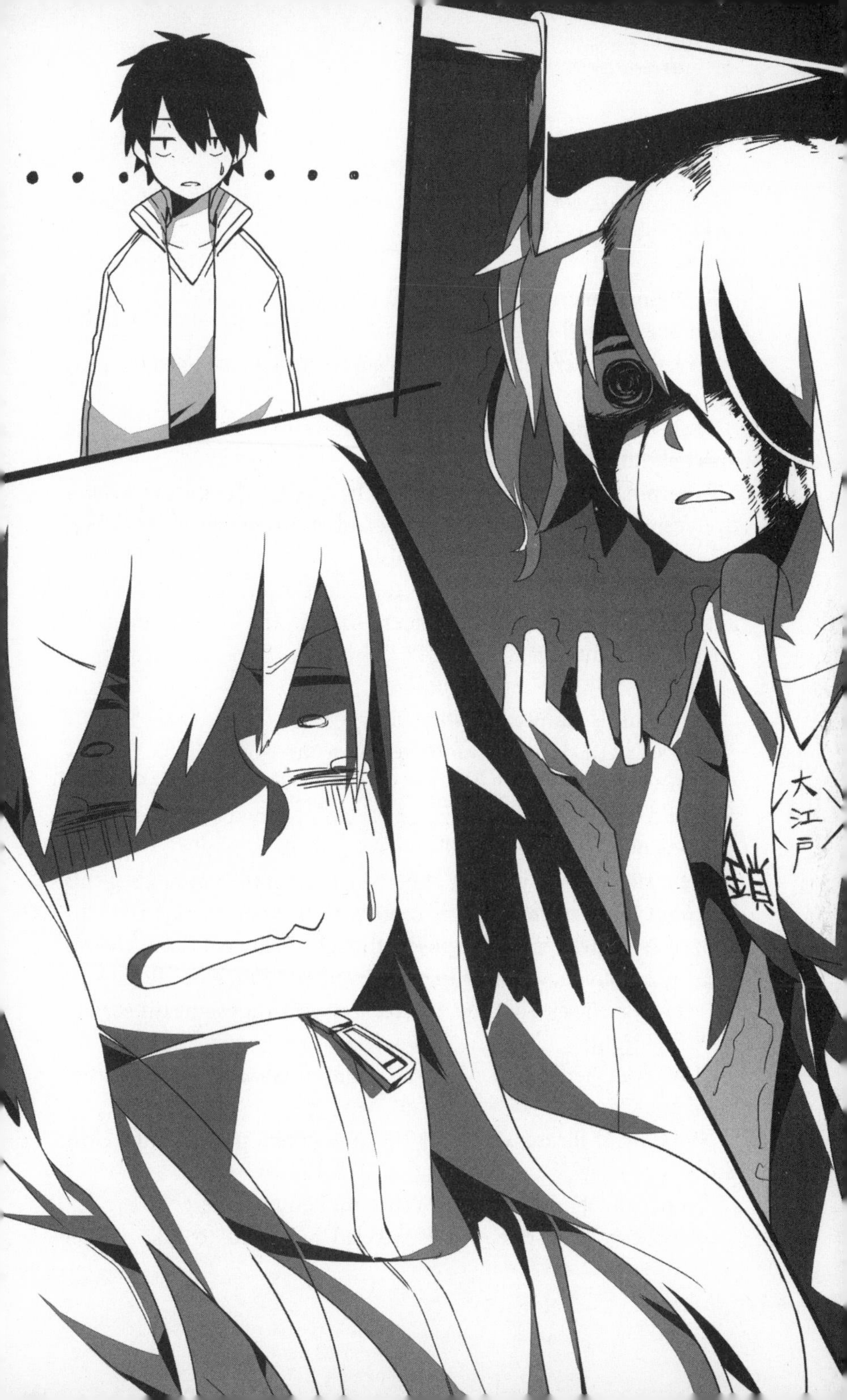
……
大江戸
鎖

"Oh, no, you're right! Oh, man…We need to wake up the boss…"

Momo began to violently jostle Kido's body.

"No, I mean, get that junk off your face first, Momo! She's gonna faint all over again if you don't!"

"Oh! Right!"

Realizing the critical flaw behind her plan, Momo dove back into the mound of coffins.

If I left Kido here, it'd probably cause a huge scene once the next group of visitors showed up.

There wasn't much I could do. Reluctantly, I dragged Kido into the area behind the coffins.

Crouching down, Momo removed the axe, took out a wet napkin from her purse to remove the makeup, and began daubing it on her face.

I sat down next to her and sighed.

The moment gave me time to reflect over how my much-anticipated alone time never materialized in the end. So much for any privacy I deserved.

"Man, this is really exhausting…"

"I'm sorry…I didn't mean to get everyone worked into a frenzy over me."

Momo, her face clear of makeup, gave me an apologetic look as she took out her phone.

The wallpaper was set to a photo she took of the entire gang this morning to commemorate the resurrection of her phone. After she resized it for wallpaper purposes, though, I was cut off at the far edge of the screen, which didn't exactly fill me with glee.

"Wow, I spent a lot of time in here…but we've got some time left to have fun, right?"

Momo put her phone away and began to shake Kido's adjacent body once more.

"Boss! Boss! Please, wake up! The amusement park's gonna close on us!"

"Nnn…gh…Huh?! Kisaragi! What am I doing in here?"

Kido's eyes flew open. She swiveled her head to take in her

surroundings, apparently not remembering how Momo shocked her into unconsciousness earlier.

"Well...uh...I dunno, you just kinda fainted all of a sudden?"

I flashed a quick wink at Momo as she spoke, deliberately averting her eyes from Kido as she did.

"Really...? Well, whatever. At least you're here now, Kisaragi. Let's hurry up and get outta here."

Kido's pupils turned from black to red as she spoke.

"I'm setting it up so that just Momo's invisible. You and I need to keep going, Shintaro."

Turning my head toward where Momo was crouching down, I realized she was already gone.

If I spent a few moments to focus on the exact site, I felt like I could see the faint contours of her body, at least. But even so, that was one useful tool Kido had at her fingertips.

What kind of tools do *I* have that would compare? The power to go to a public bathhouse and not be embarrassed out of my skull?

Regardless, we headed back out into the corridor. Our mission: to reach the exit in one piece.

I could feel the onrush of depression as I realized it meant my heart would soon be working overtime again.

The moment I set foot in the hallway, I suddenly felt a strange sense that something wasn't quite right.

It was something that had taken up residence in my mind ever since we ran into Momo. But once I gave it some thought, I immediately realized the cause.

No. Wait a second. If *that* was the case, does that mean this entire afternoon was...?

A bitter chill ran down my spine as it dawned on me. I decided to bounce the idea off the already-trembling Kido.

I stopped in the middle of the corridor. She followed suit.

"…Hmm? What's up, Shintaro? Let's get going."

Yep…I hated to think about it, but my hunch was probably right. In a way, I had already unconsciously confirmed it earlier.

"Hey…Kido? After Ene rode the roller coaster…where'd she go after that?"

Kido flashed me a confused expression.

"Ene? She left right afterward. She said she'd be following you."

—As she spoke, the phone in my pocket vibrated for two quick bursts, as if chuckling to itself.

*

I was seated by myself on a bench.

"Aaaaaaahggghghhh!! My hooooooodiiiieeeee!!"

That haunted house was pretty frightening at first, but the second half wasn't that bad at all.

Yep. Just a plain old amusement-park attraction. Nothing too rough.

After we escaped, Momo and Kido went off by themselves to round up the rest of our gang, promising to contact me later on.

The two other males in our group were one thing, but considering Marie probably didn't have her own phone, I figured they'd need a fair amount of time.

"Aaaaaaaaahhhhh!! I'm sorry, I'm sorry! Please, let me go!!"

In the end, the private time I had lusted after so badly was nothing but an illusion.

That's what I get for trying to spread my wings a little…This is just pitiful.

* * *

"Ngh...Oh, man, I don't feel too good...Urk...urggh..."
"—Aaagghh!! Stop it! Stop playing that back!!"

My patience finally met its match. After I shouted at my phone, a blue-haired, twin-ponytailed girl appeared on-screen, flailing her legs in the air as she rolled around on the floor laughing.

"Ooooh, my stomach hurts...! Aw, I'm really sorry, master. But, I mean, you've been giving me all this hilarious material today, so... Bah hah hah hah!!"
"I'm not your 'material,' Ene! Ughh...If I knew *you* were here with me, I would've sealed up my mouth with duct tape..."

"Yeeaaaggghhhh!! Aaaaaarrrgghh!! You scared me!! What the hell?! I'm sorry, I'm sorry!!...Oh, man, I don't feel too good..."

Here I was, already cast forlornly against the rocks of despair, and meanwhile Ene was cracking herself up building a soundboard of my greatest screams to play around with.

She had been inside my phone ever since I was speaking with Kano and Seto on that bench earlier. She had taken advantage of this to record audio and video of every lowlight of the day, and now it was the latest plaything she was addicted to.

"Oh, man, I can hardly breathe any longer...Whew! Anyway, master! Did you have fun today?"

The question was innocent enough, the smile as her head occupied the entire screen happy enough, but I couldn't sense a trace of goodwill on her face.

"...Yeah...thanks to you, it was the worst day of my life. Thanks a bunch."

I had grown used to this treatment. I fully understood that flying into a rage would do nothing to improve my lot in life.

But I still gripped the handset with so much force, I'm surprised I didn't crack the display.

"Oh, no, no need to thank me! Besides…I haven't had a chance to play around at all today! We still got a lot of spots to visit, you know!"

"Huhh?! Come on, you *have* to be tired out by now, right?! Let's just go home…"

"Nothing doing! I haven't even had the slightest iota of fun! You promised that you'd be together with me, master. Don't think that I've forgotten that!"

Ene puffed up her face, the same way she always did when attempting to threaten me.

I've been through this pattern before. She gets all mad, I say whatever comes to mind to try to deal with it, and I wind up paying for it big-time later on.

One time, a while ago, she invited me to play this online game with her.

My intention was to ignore her request from start to finish, but immediately afterward, I found my computer infested with viruses of every possible kind. She agreed to root them out, as long as I agreed to play with her…and pay for whatever extra in-game items she felt like she needed.

…Contemplating all the crap I always have to deal with after every decision, it'd probably be smarter to make sure she doesn't get angry at me in the first place.

But, man, what a pain in the…

"…If you don't take me around the park with you, I'll show your folder of innermost secrets to your sister…"

"All *righty!* I am *pumped* to have some *fun!!* What should we tackle first, huh? Anything without a lot of G-forces is A-OK with me!"

Well, time to see this through to the end. I stood up off the bench and looked at Ene. She looked eminently satisfied, gloating in the wake of her latest victory.

It was a fact, though, that I hadn't yet really enjoyed my first planned outing in years, either.

Having to share it with her pained me, but hey, we *were* in an amusement park.

I didn't really mind checking out some of the attractions a bit longer.

"Aw, that's great to hear, master! What should we start with…? Oh! How about that thing? The one where you sit on a chair and blast away at aliens! You're really good at shooters and stuff, right, master?"

"Uh? How do you know *that?* Have we ever played a shooter together?"

"Oh, no? Guess not. Well, like it matters. I know everything about you, master! Let's just get going already, okay?"

Ene whipped out a finger to navigate for me.

"All right…Whatever. You're the boss. Just try not to cause a scene, okay…?"

"You got it!"

Ene was all smiles as she answered.

She was utterly self-centered,

completely wicked,

and absolutely impossible to get a grasp of.

Something about the observation made a memory from the past reach the tip of my tongue, but I trundled it away before giving it any more thought.

Right now, my mind was already fully occupied trying to deal with this girl and her high-maintenance ego.

—How much fun can we have before sunset?

I held my mobile phone like a compass and started walking in the direction Ene pointed.

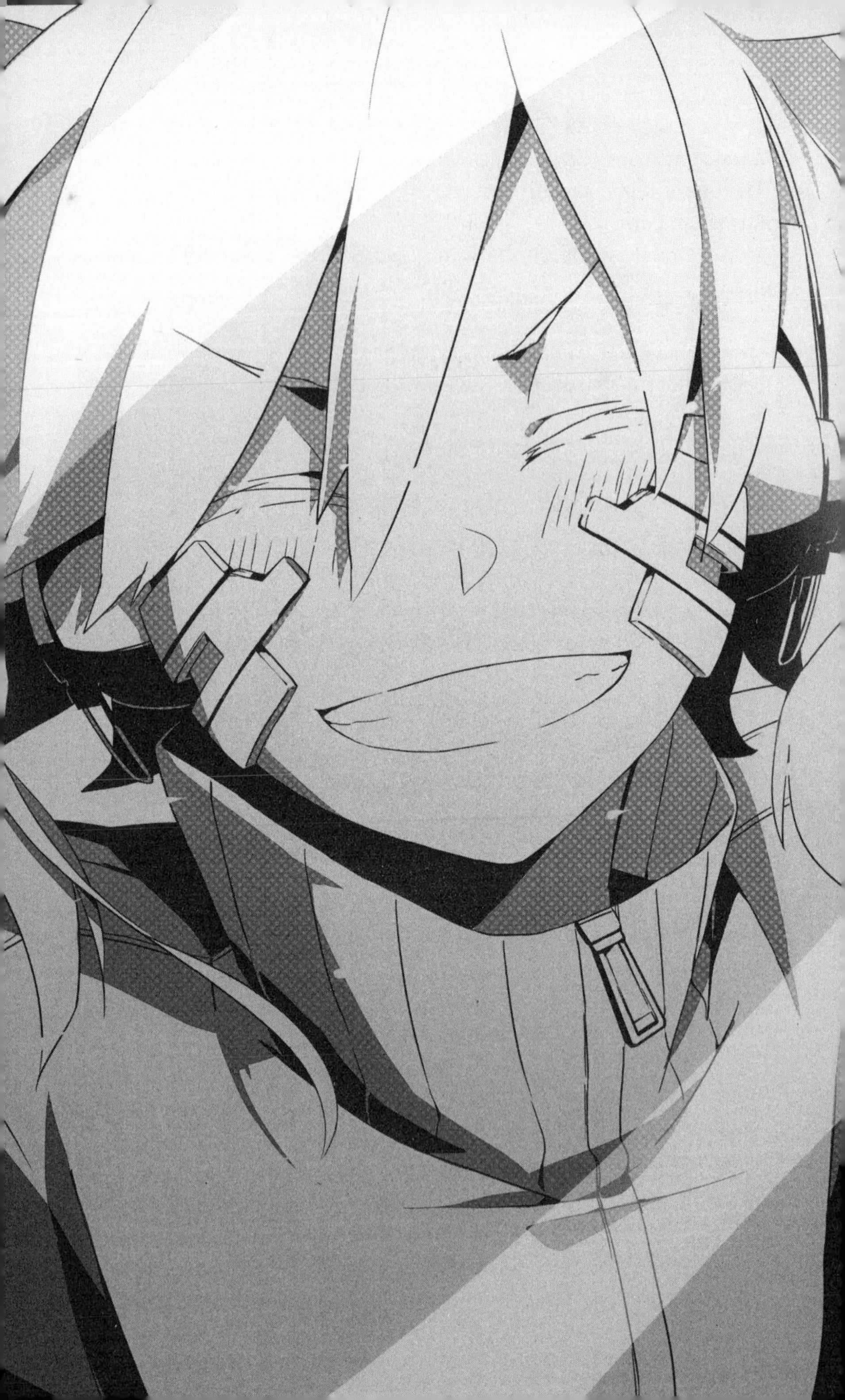

AFTERWORD

"Too Terrible to Look At"

Hello. Jin speaking.

Did you enjoy *Kagerou Daze 2: A Headphone Actor*?

This novel was written in the middle of summer, with the temperature outside never going below the upper eighties—not unlike the story setting I was writing about. Of course, I had the AC set to seventy-three degrees and gorged myself on pizza throughout the project, but the point remains.

I apologize for leeching off everyone at the office in the meantime.

Which reminds me. In the afterword to my previous novel, *Kagerou Daze: In a Daze*, I wrote something along the lines of "If this winds up being a flop, I'll have to write a school romance/comedy next!" Luckily, thanks to all of you, the response I received for that book exceeded all expectations. Thanks! *smile*

As a result, the manifesto above is not the reason why this volume wound up being a bit school romance/comedy-ish.

The real reason is simply that I have grown starved for affection. Rest assured about that, please!

This volume, much like the last, was written in the midst of a busy schedule of music composing and live concerts. But it was no big deal…as long as you consider a breakneck, death-march schedule that made me feel like I was about to froth at the mouth no big deal.

No, no, it really wasn't hard at all, you know? It's true.

Just thinking about starting work on Volume 3 gets me so excited, it makes me want to release everything I've eaten today right into the toilet!

My HP gauge, which has gradually been falling over time, recently went from yellow to red and flashing.

I'm writing this Volume 2 afterword right after finishing the novel, amidst what I could only call a hazy sense of consciousness. I'm afraid I'm going to mess up and write something dirty without even realizing it. It makes me, and my big, luscious double Ds that just won't quit, terribly frightened.

Though I really don't have to worry. I'm sure my editor (Ikebo) will clean up and de-curse everything before it reaches the readers' hands, after all. I know he will. Yep.

(* Editor's note: This afterword is being published as-is per author request.)

Speaking of dirty jokes, the way I kept writing "chin chin" (the name of a rose variety, not the name of a certain body part) in the last volume's afterword nowadays makes me cringe every time my mom out in the country (age fifty-two) calls me up and says, "I'm telling everyone I know that my son's written a novel, all right? So keep up the good work!"

And yet, when my sister (age eighteen) told me, "You've be surprised how many of my friends are reading it!" I was instead filled with an alarming sense of excitement.

Hey, sister's friends, are you reading this? Yeah, I'm that girl's brother! *grin*

My sister also tells me I resemble Shintaro, the novel character, a lot.

I can't say I agree with her, and to be frank I consider Shintaro to be a pretty gross and distasteful character overall, so I was less than thrilled with this assessment. But then I took another perspective.

*   *   *

Maybe, just maybe, I could take advantage of this.

If I had Shintaro get friendly with some women in the novel, maybe that'd help me get a little more lovin' attention from the ladies around me in real life. No, it *has* to! I'm sure! Maybe!

I mean, remember how Shintaro busted up his PC in Volume 1? My computer just crashed and burned, too, giving me some kind of indecipherable error as it did. You have to admit it—there's some kind of deep, intertwined connection going on here.

Thus, Shintaro has more than a little bit of fun in this volume. So there you go. I'll be expecting someone to send me amusement-park tickets in the mail before long. I can't wait!

Along similar lines, I've been sitting every day at my PC, pants down, wondering if today's the day when a cute girl will appear on-screen, start talking to me, and never go away for *me*, too. But there's no sign of her yet, weirdly. Why? It honestly baffles me.

The other day, though, I stumbled upon an ad for an adult site that, no matter how many times I closed it, kept on popping up anyway.

This isn't exactly how I imagined things would unfold, but I've been keeping my mental state stable lately by talking to this ad on a daily basis. Thanks, God.

Well, it's just about time to say my good-byes again for now.

I received gracious support from all kinds of wonderful people as I wrote this volume. Thanks very much for that.

Also, thanks in advance to my readers for their continued support, of course!

Let's meet up in the afterword to Volume 3, all right? See you—'till then!

Jin (Shizen no Teki-P)

My apologies.

This is Sidu; good to see you again.
I'm responsible for the illustrations
once again in this novel, something
which I'm very thankful for.
I figured I'd draw a really cool
picture of Shintaro for this page,
just like I talked about in the
previous book, but since I have
even less time now than I did back
then, I'm giving you a really cool
drawing of a sesame seed instead.
I've deceived you with a seed.
I've de-seeded you. Uh....
Sorry about that.
Again, thanks very much.

Really cool
sesame seed

9/14/2012
Sidu

celebratory comments

Great work, guys!

Congratulations on releasing the second volume! It's been just as fun to read this time around!

I just love the world Jin's created, to say nothing of Sidu's artwork!! Ene and Konoha were both really cute in this volume! Kido, too! Oh, and Kano! But there isn't enough **Hibiya** in this book. The same goes for **Marie** and **Seto**, too. And so...

Here you go!

Congratulations on releasing the second volume of Kagerou Daze! With this volume, the plot is centered around the tune "Headphone Actor," which is my favorite out of all of them, so I'm really excited to see how the story unfolds.
I'm sure things are going to stay busy for all of you, so watch you don't work yourselves too hard...!!

Ishiburo

Masterrr!

It's me, Ene!

VOLUME 2!!
CONGRATULATIONS!!

THIS IS RYUSE. IF YOU DON'T KNOW ME, GOOD TO MEET YOU! BIG CONGRATS GO OUT TO JIN, SIDU, AND WANNYAN FOR GETTING THE SECOND NOVEL VOLUME PUBLISHED! BOY, YOU MUST HAVE GONE THROUGH A LOT FOR IT, HUH? MYSELF, I'VE BEEN THROUGH SO MUCH LATELY, I'VE TRANSFORMED FROM A MOMO FANBOY TO A MARIE FANBOY. (CHECK OUT MY NOTE IN VOLUME 1 FOR MORE ON THAT.) ANYWAY, I HOPE YOU GUYS KEEP ON TRUCKING! I'LL BE CHEERING YOU ON!

MARIE, INCORRECT ← FOREST-GIRL VERSION

RYUSE

MEOWWW!

keep on pushing and get as far as you can with it!!

I'll be looking on at an angle from behind.

Aka Akasaka
(the IA Vocaloid guy)

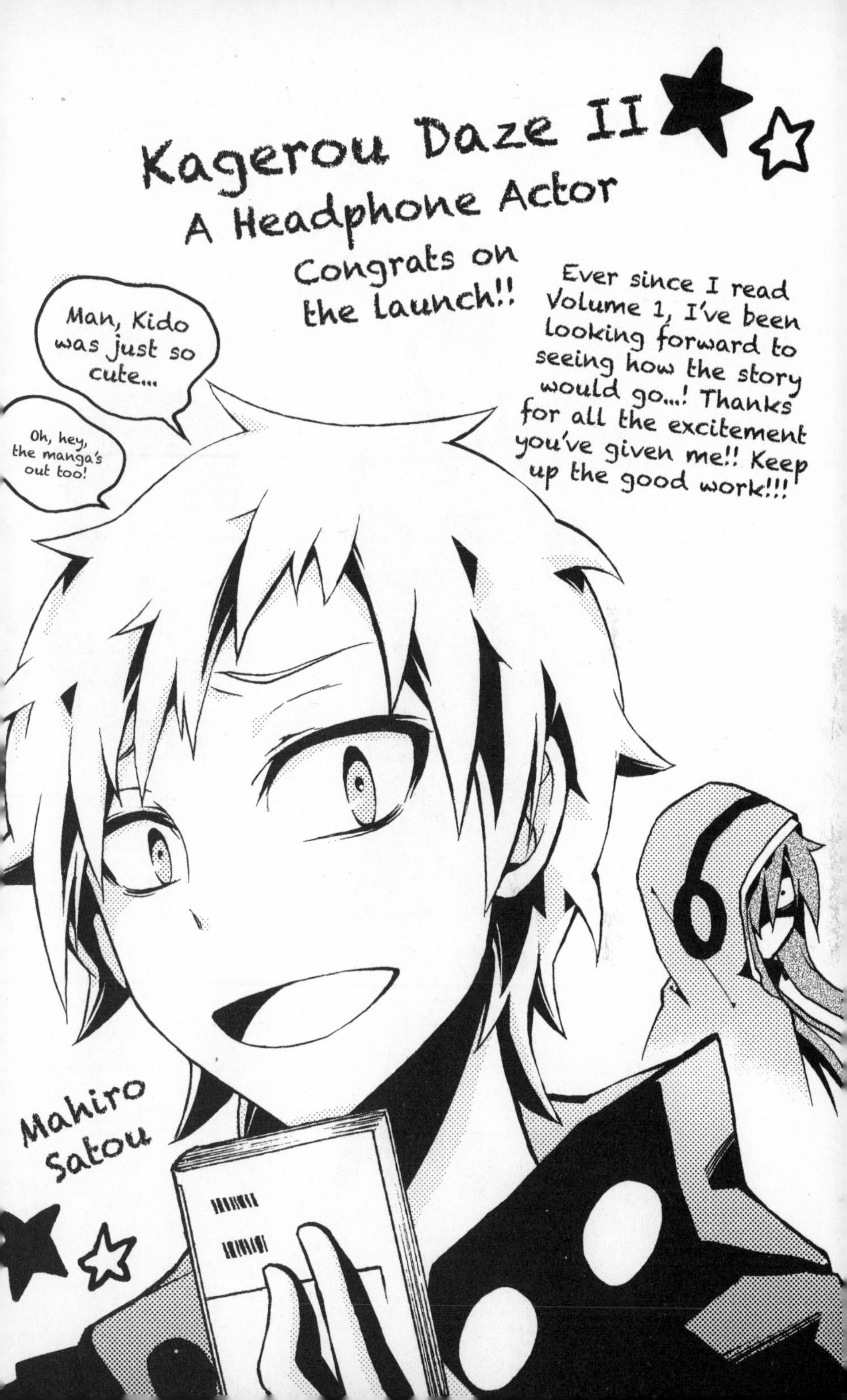
Kagerou Daze II
A Headphone Actor
Congrats on the launch!!
Ever since I read Volume 1, I've been looking forward to seeing how the story would go...! Thanks for all the excitement you've given me!! Keep up the good work!!!
Man, Kido was just so cute...
Oh, hey, the manga's out too!
Mahiro Satou

—MODEL SHEETS—

Seto

accidentally made
him look kinda Shota

Kano probably
calls him
"froggie"

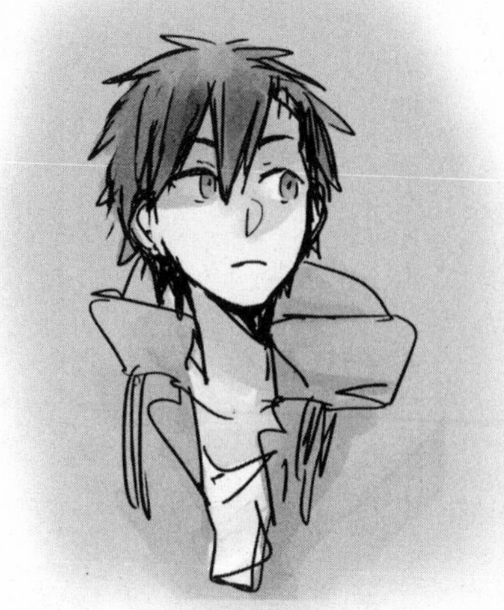

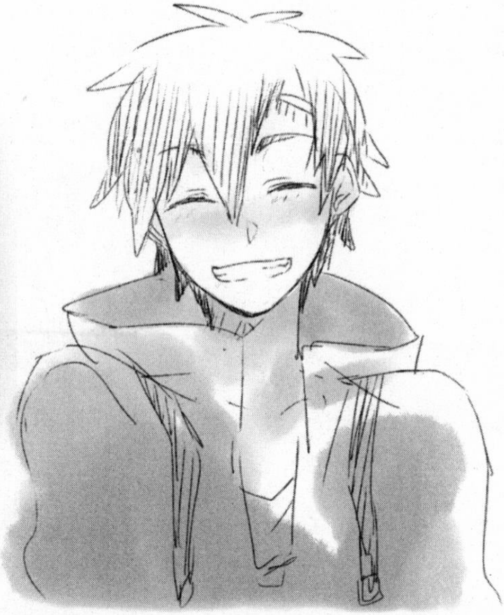

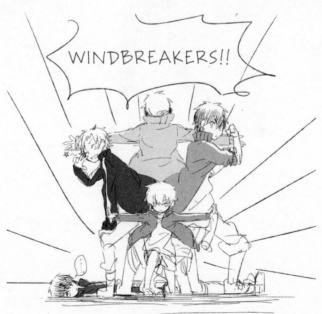

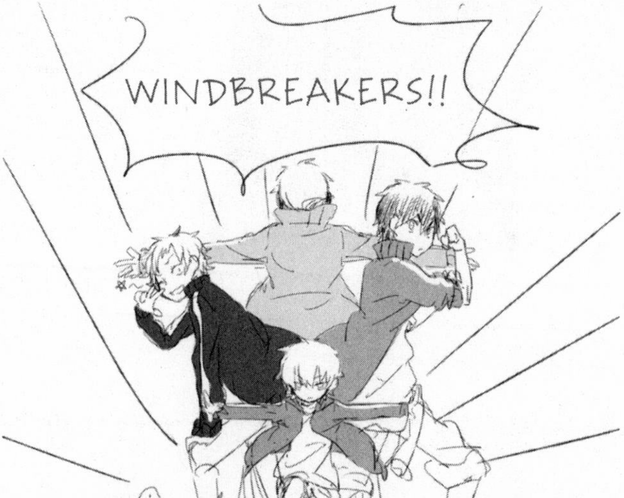
WINDBREAKERS!!

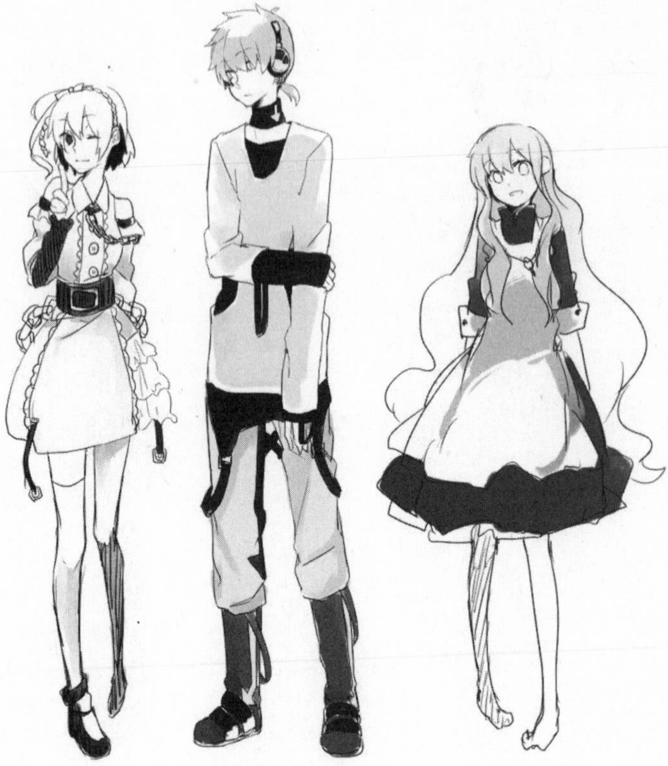

MOMO KONOHA MARIE

CAST OF CHARACTERS

ENE　　　**SHINTARO**　　　**AYANO**

KANO   AZAMI   KENJIROU TATEYAMA

CAST OF CHARACTERS ↘

HIBIYA   **HIYORI**   **KIDO**

SCHOOL UNIFORM DESIGNS

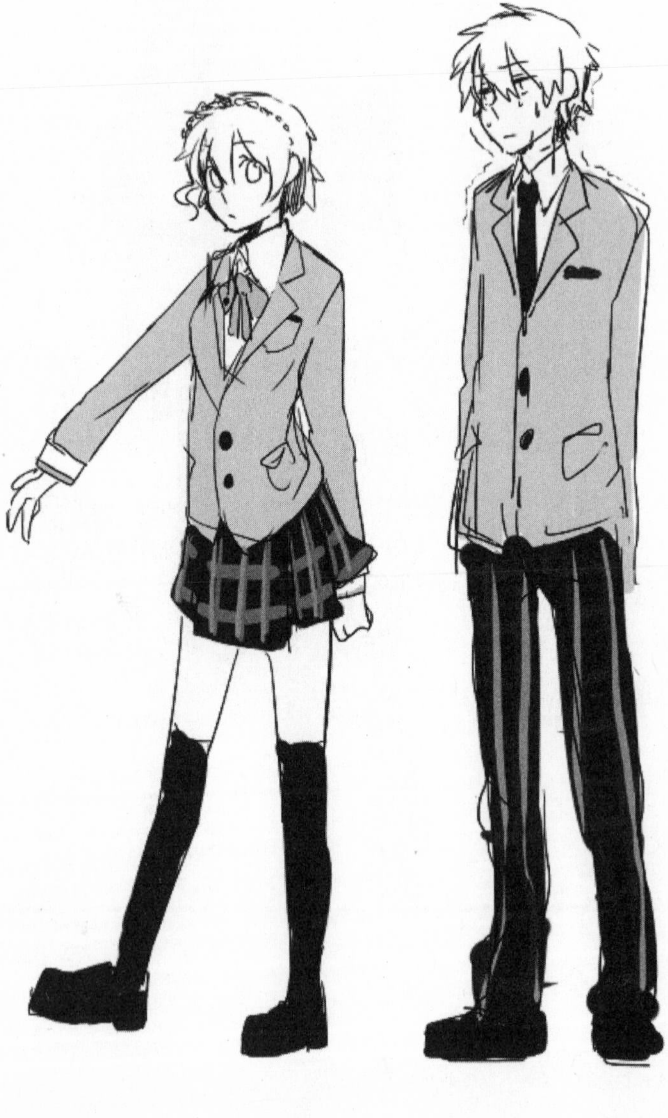

past
Ene

past

beauty
mark